'Very dark, very funny and very original. Helen FitzGerald is one of a kind, and a welcome breath of fresh air in the world of off-beat but achingly relatable crime fiction' SJI Holliday

'I'm convinced that Helen FitzGerald is some kind of genius. *Worst Case Scenario* is dark, unsettling, shocking and brilliantly funny – often at the same time. It also confirms her as queen of the killer opening line. Loved it' Paul Burston

'Oh. My. God. This was just wow. Razor-sharp, smart, shocking, dark, and amazingly executed. I wanna watch *Sex and the City* with Mary!' Louise Beech

'I can't think of another book that had me laughing out loud on the one hand and gripped, worrying what would happen next on the other. It's a skill. I did want to throw the book against the wall at the end … But that's a result in terms of reader engagement!' Heleen Kist

'This book took me on such a journey and a range of emotions! Laughing, cringing and hesitant all at the same time. Also very grateful I never became a social worker. Totally gripping and so well written' Madeleine Black

'Twisted and utterly contemporary, this is pure, unfiltered noir. From that killer opening line to the dark irony of its final scene. You need to read this' Russel McLean

'The BEST opening to a book I have ever read. Hooked? You bet!' The Writing Garnet

'The harrowing plot keeps you gripped until the final, devastating revelation' Deirdre O'Brien, *Sunday Mirror*

'A book you find yourself greedily gulping down' Teddy Jamieson, *Herald Scotland*

'Already being hailed as this year's talking-point novel for parents – the equivalent of *The Slap* … A gripping read [that] will hit a nerve' Helen Rumbelow, *The Times*

'My hat is totally off to this writer' Laura Lippman

'Brilliant … three hundred pages of taut, sharp, chilling and often laugh-out-loud funny genius' Lisa Jewell

'Extraordinary. In a just universe, it will be Helen FitzGerald's *Gone Girl* moment. Read it at once' Steve Mosby

'In this very modern novel, which arrives at a startling conclusion, FitzGerald manipulates our knowledge of earlier cases in which women have been wrongly accused' Joan Smith, *Sunday Times*

'FitzGerald's punchy thriller fleshes out new circles of parental hell' Emma Hagestadt, *Independent*

'Exceptional … this powerful noir tale is by turns devastating and uplifting' Chris Ewan

'A book that is so psychologically astute and well written at the level of the sentence. It is good to know that bestsellers don't have to be stupid' Nicholas Lezard, *Guardian*

'A real psychological roller coaster … enhanced, too, by some pleasingly gritty, choppy dialogue and smatterings of FitzGerald's signature dark humour, making it highly readable' Emily Hunnisett, *Scotsman*

'Brilliant, shocking and unputdownable' *Sydney Morning Herald*

'Funny, moving, horrifying and compelling' *Times Literary Supplement*

'Satisfyingly shocking' *Big Issue*

'FitzGerald's experiences in social work lend her novels piercing insight and breath-taking authenticity … chilling, absorbing storylines littered with disturbing truths, dark humour and spine-tingling tensions' *Lancashire Evening Post*

WORST CASE SCENARIO

WORST CASE SCENARIO

HELEN FITZGERALD

**ORENDA
BOOKS**

Orenda Books
16 Carson Road
West Dulwich
London SE21 8HU
www.orendabooks.co.uk

First published in the United Kingdom by Orenda Books, 2019
Copyright © Helen FitzGerald, 2019

A catalogue record for this book is available from the British Library.

ISBN 978-1-912374-69-4
eISBN 978-1-912374-70-0

Typeset in Garamond by MacGuru Ltd
Printed and bound by
CPI Group (UK) Ltd, Croydon, CR0 4YY

For sales and distribution, please contact *info@orendabooks.co.uk*

To criminal-justice social workers,
who do the hardest job and have the best chat

WORST CASE SCENARIO

PART ONE

THE WIFE KILLER

1

Every time Mary tried to relax in a bath, a paedophile ruined it. Tonight it was McKinley, who she'd visited on the way home, and who had sat on the sofa for ten minutes with one or more balls hanging out of his shorts. She still wasn't sure if it was deliberate. Probably not, as Mary was fifty-two, not five. 'I'm not allowed to think about that,' Mary said out loud, and McKinley's ball/s disappeared into the bubbles.

As ever, another case invaded immediately – not a sex offender, but a far more palatable wife killer who she'd be meeting for the first time tomorrow. Ten years ago, Dr Liam Macdowall took his beloved wife to Loch Fyne for oysters and on the way home, drove the car off a bridge. A lot of 'murder-suicides' seemed to end this way – with one party still alive, usually the prick whose idea it was. Mary put her head under water and called on her victim-empathy skills, imagining she was Macdowall's dead wife, Bella:

Liam's in the car beside me, belted in as I am. The water's rising and I'm running out of breath. Please do something because I can't get out. He's undoing his seatbelt. Why won't mine budge? I can't define the look he gives me – is it love? – before he forces his way out of the car.

Mary lifted her head out of the bathwater, took a deep breath, and repeated: 'I must not think about that.' This mantra had helped keep her sane enough. Home was precious; work must not invade. I must not think about that: a sacred rule that was impossible to obey, and the only one she wanted to.

The next morning, Mary pressed her ID against the flex machine. She was forty-one hours up. If she didn't use the hours by the end of the month, which was today, they would be wiped. She wanted to smash the machine with her forehead. Instead she ruminated as she gathered the paperwork for the prison meeting: *Fucking management. Fucking job.*

Mary's respect for her impoverished employer had been dissipating for years but had slipped substantially over the last week. It was a week ago that Mary was scolded by her boss's boss for allegedly breaching flexitime rules. The inciting incident involved lunch, which workers were required to take, even though there was no time, no where, and no thing to eat. If workers didn't clock in and out at lunchtime, they were docked an extra thirty minutes. Mary's 'pod' of six therefore removed their IDs from their necks at noon and took turns to go downstairs and flex each other in and out. It was a futile exercise, as no-one ever had time to take the minutes they saved, but it provided some comfort. Once rage-filled poverty-busters, Mary and her pod now rebelled by pooling lanyards at noon.

'What are you doing?' Mary's boss's boss, Shirley, had said when she caught her gang-pinging the machine seven days previously.

Mary had been getting red-mist attacks for eighteen months and could feel one coming on. Weight-related insults screamed within. She had to suppress them.

'It's prohibited to use another person's ID,' Shirley had said.

'Is it?' Mary continued to ping. 'Look how many hours I'm up, and there's no way for me to use them.'

'In that case, what's the point in what you're doing, Mary?'

Using someone's name in a sentence should be banned. 'Mary' hung there for seconds before she said, 'It's all right for you, *Shirley*. You obviously have plenty of time to eat lunch.'

Oops.

Because of that incident, a meeting was being convened by Shirley and Mary's boss to discuss the potential need for an urgent meeting with Mary.

News quickly spread throughout the office. Mary was a Registered Flex Offender.

She was also at stage three in terms of sickness. Stage three was a terrible thing to be at, apparently. Colleagues took sharp intakes of breath when Mary told them she was at stage three. Mary had spread, she could metastasise, and die. If she took another sick day this year – and it was only halfway through – very, very bad things would happen.

No-one took sick leave anymore. Apart from anything, the workers were terrified that others would get a chance to look into their cases then out them as lazy and shit. Lil had come in with pneumonia the previous year and fainted in the loo, but only Mary knew. Helena shared terrible infections with her pod almost weekly, and Jeff had come in two days after breaking one leg, two arms and his collarbone in a car accident on the way back from Troon Live. He needed three support workers to help him write court reports and go to the loo, but his sickness record was impeccable.

So far this year, Mary's sick leave totalled seven days, but that was enough to be stage three. The first day was to go to the doctor. For months, she'd been moody and rage-filled and ruminating and tired, so tired. Someone had unscrewed the top of her head and poured wet cement in; glug, glug, glug, she explained to the young male GP. It was surprising how much room she had inside for wet cement. And then it set, and she was immovable. When someone wanted her attention – Mary! Call for you Mary, Jimmy McKinley in reception for you Mary, Mary, Mum, Mary! – a huge concrete drill zzzz-ed at her casing: deafening, echoing, shuddering, cracking at her chest: MARY!

The young male GP gave her antidepressants.

Which caused sick days two, three and four, and her escalation to stage two. Mary had never felt less herself than while she was on Prozac. She didn't understand the world. She couldn't hear herself speak. She felt the anxiety, but she wasn't thinking it. She poured sweat, she smelt, she gained five pounds.

Days five, six and seven were spent weaning herself off the pills, rocking in bed wondering if she was uncannily similar to Virginia Woolf. She suspected not; she suspected she'd have just taken the rocks out of her pockets and swum back. Also, fiction was pointless in Mary's opinion. No-one ever told stories as wild and upsetting as the ones that happened for real in Renfield.

The flex incident one week earlier was indeed inciting. Mary decided, *Fuck it, I'm giving notice. Now Roddie's hit the big time, I'm gonna knit poufs and have a proper go at tap-dancing.* She had narrowly escaped a thorough sacking and would resign with her record intact. She would leave with her head held high.

Mary arrived at the prison with two minutes to spare. Officer MacDonald (one of the 'badduns', rumour had it) tagged her from gate to wall to gate and deposited her at the ICM Suite. She'd been to these meetings many times, and the feeling of dread in her tummy was always justified, but even more so today, because Liam Macdowall was famous. His 'book' – *Cuck: Letters to My Dead Wife* – was being released on the same day as his person, which is why he had invited his 'publisher', Derek McLaverty to the meeting.

Derek was twenty-nine, skinny, bookish (i.e., could read), and a leading Men's Rights Activist (MRA). Written in black lettering on his white t-shirt were the words: *THIS IS WHAT A MRA LOOKS LIKE.* Mary had an immediate chemical reaction to the guy. He reminded her of Thomas McInnes at St Pat's, who spread rumours about her when she beat him at spelling and who chased her round Queen's Park a few years later to finger her, spreading worse rumours cos she got away.

Derek was her childhood nemesis on steroids. He oozed self-satisfaction. At the coffee stand Mary said: 'It should be "*an* MRA". The article is decided by pronunciation. But I've read your blog, so I know grammar's not your thing.'

'You've read my blog? I'm flattered.' Derek hailed himself as a 'proud Scot' but he was educated at Gordonstoun and spoke like Prince Charles would if Prince Charles was trying not to speak like Prince Charles. His blog was called The Lion's Roar. Mary couldn't read it for more than three seconds without needing alcohol. The guy had a face you'd never tire of slapping, probably why his mama sent him to the Highlands to build rafts, hone sexism and puff his chest about the Union. When his father's dotcom business went downhill, Derek was forced to leave boarding school. He travelled 'extensively', meeting and marrying Pretty Pam from Renfield, who was beneath him in every way except reality (now rid of him, she wore heels whenever she wanted). They shared five years together, all of them unhappy according to his social worker, Nel. Their two boys, Freddie (four) and Oskar (two), now lived with their battered mother and her parents, and Derek spent most of his time arguing – as publicly as possible – that he should be allowed to see them whenever he wanted, at the same time as failing to attend supervised contact week after week, leaving the wee lads sobbing in a sad room on the ground floor of Kenneth House. Derek's brief career with the police force had been brought to an abrupt halt after his first conviction for domestic assault, but he continued to ooze authority with mind-blowing arrogance. Mary already hated Derek more than anyone she'd ever met, and she'd met the Symington Strangler, but that was another story.

Macdowall had invited his lawyer as well, who didn't need to be on the personal invite list, plus a balding alcohol counsellor called Tracy and his twenty-six-year-old daughter, Holly.

Six days earlier, Mary had visited Holly to compile a way-overdue home background report. It was a day after she'd made her decision to resign. For one freeing day, she had stopped thinking of herself as a social worker. Her boundaries, which had been withering for a while, were almost totally gone, and it was wonderful. Speaking her mind didn't seem dangerous at all.

'Your father's asked if he can stay here,' she explained to

Holly. 'Apparently you're okay with that. How 'bout you make us tea and we get these questions out of the way? I'm white with one.' She paused and looked at the kettle.

Holly looked at the kettle as well, then at her. 'I'm uncomfortable with your expectation of tea.'

Mary didn't flinch. 'Would you like to make a formal complaint?'

'What? *No.*'

Mary had already set out her notepad and pen on the table. She dated the fresh, lined page then deadpanned: 'Tea's gonna help with rapport.'

One lengthy silence later, Holly put on the kettle.

'Gingernut?' Mary fished two dodgy-looking biscuits from her cavernous fabric bag then removed her jumper.

Holly did not want a biscuit.

'Tell me about yourself.' Chewing, Mary made a rolling motion with her hand to start things off. 'E.g., "I was born…"'

Mary's bag was open on the floor, so Holly could see the book inside. 'You got a proof copy?'

'As part of his prison dossier. Read it in two sittings,' Mary said.

'What did you think?' Clearly expecting high praise, Holly sipped her tea and seemed to relax.

'Load of shite. I'd prefer to share a house with Hannibal Lecter. No matter what you say to me today, I'm gonna recommend that your father should not live with you under any circumstances.'

'Who's your manager?'

'My senior's name is…' Mary jotted the name and number of her boss on a council issue *With Compliments* slip, then reached into her bag for an A4 piece of paper headed 'Official

Complaint Form'. 'Her name's Catherine Buteman, and she will agree with your complaint wholeheartedly. Now, where were we?'

Holly reached down and pulled the book out of Mary's bag. She touched the cover, which the picture of her dad's face filled. The title was across his chest, with the letter C embroidered in red on his t-shirt: *Cuck: Letters to My Dead Wife*, by Dr Liam Macdowall.

'Doctor.' Mary sniggered a tad. 'Of what again?'

'Geography.'

'Haha.' Her laugh was accidental.

'What's funny about geography?'

Mary thought about it a while and then laughed again. 'Oh, come on, you know it just is.' She blew her nose until all the laugh came out. 'He never did use it though, did he?'

'Mum's job came first. Mostly he looked after me.' Holly's face was burning red. 'In your day it was okay to talk about a man like he's nothing. You don't know my father.'

'I know hundreds of him.' Mary stared the girl out; a battle of the generations. 'Do you want revenge – is that why you're putting in all this work to have him here?' Holly's impressive suburban terrace had been painted and renovated within an inch of its life. 'Have you been planning this for years?'

Holly was filling in the complaint form, and honed in on the employee number on Mary's ID – *84737*.

'It's *84787*. The second eight's smudged. Merlot I think. Looks like a three but it's an eight. That's right, good. So, Daddy gets out, and you make him pay by nagging him while you poison him slowly. Or is your plan to unman him all over again – how do you *un-man* a superhero like your father? *MISOGNY MAN! Can demoralise a woman with a single glance.*'

'My mother managed.'

'You think your mother emasculated your father?'

'He couldn't find work in Glasgow.'

'What a bitch.'

'Are you going through the change?' Holly had taken Mary's sarcasm and raised it one fuck-you.

What was that rising from Mary's belly: heat? 'I've always been like this.' She wasn't sure if she was lying.

'Mmhmm,' judged the girl. 'I caught her at it two years earlier, you know that? Night before my fourteenth – got up as usual to see if my presents were in the lounge and if one was bike-shaped. Heard her whispering in her office, so I peeked in thinking she might be wrapping it, but she was Skyping a hairy dude with her top off. She promised not to do it again if I promised not to tell. So, for two years I lied to him, the person I loved most in the world. Can you imagine what it felt like? And she kept on doing it.'

'You think your mother was a *whore*?'

The girl shook her head; not a no, not a yes.

'Fair enough then, eh? Drown the slut.'

Holly put her pen down. 'I'm gonna need a bigger form.'

A vision of pink-haired Mary intruded: twenty-five, all hopey and carey and believing the things clients told her. Pink-haired Mary would never get herself into this situation, and if she did she'd be shitting herself. *A complaint? Oh my God, sorry. What have I done; what should I do?* Intrusive thought. Mary banished it.

'I was very *good* at my job for over twenty-nine years,' she said. 'I was all – "and how does that make you *feel*?" – but yesterday I decided to leave, which means I don't have to pretend to care anymore and I don't have time to manipulate you into seeing the truth. I've decided to be bad at this job.

My guess is that I'll be much better at it when I'm bad at it. Being good has rather held me back. Your father's dangerous; tell him to get to fuck.'

'I'd rather tell you.'

'Practise on me.'

Holly stood and pointed in the direction of fuck. 'Get to fuck.'

Mary was unmoved. 'See how easy that was. You're a doormat, a classic victim. You're: *I don't matter. You matter.* The type who says to your more-significant other: *I don't mind, what would you like for lunch? Of course, you go out and have fun, honey. I'll see if I can get enough hot water to take a bath!* Or *Come and live with me, Daddy. I'll cook for you.*'

'Dad's a great cook.'

'You'll do the cooking because it's dull, and you don't matter and he does. Why on earth are you still in this big house on your own? In these rooms filled with hatred and death? I can feel it. It's yours now, not his. Sell it. Get out of here. Go live in Auckland, or Peru. You don't even work, do you? Don't even need to? Buy a one-way ticket somewhere. Leave.'

Holly may well have been taking this in. Hard to tell. She'd sat back down and was staring at the complaint form, not writing anything.

'What's scary is the *I don't matter* type of person snaps in the end. The wife takes it and takes it, then one night she finds herself drugging her man's hot chocolate and chopping his dick off when he's sleeping. The girlfriend takes it and takes it, then one night she's washing and he's drying, and she's smashing him over the head with a Le Creuset.'

Holly looked up, finally. 'A what-say?'

'A really heavy saucepan.'

'I *do* matter.' Holly stood up again. 'And I need you to leave.'

'Then behave like you matter.' Mary began packing the large number of items she'd deposited around her in the last fifteen minutes. 'Your life not miserable enough? What do you do besides smoke bongs? Yes, I can smell it. It's not like you're Catholic. You don't have to forgive him.'

Holly signed the thoroughly completed complaint form and took on her stare. 'I'll be requesting a different worker.'

'I'm not your *worker*.'

Holly shooed her to the door, tried to shepherd her out. 'Hopefully not, but what you are – definitely – is damaged, dated, and a bigot.'

Holly hadn't looked at Mary once since they took their seats in the ICM suite. Her hatred had obviously matured over the last six days.

Mary's, on the other hand, had evaporated. Holly was just a vulnerable young girl, drowning here in a sea of testostefuck. Mary should never have done the home background interview in the mood she was in, but there were good reasons for her straight talking; it was tough love. Could the girl not see they were on the same side?

At the head of the table, as if he was prime minister, sat *Dr* Liam Macdowall, chatting away to the alcohol counsellor like they were old pals. This felt more like a marketing meeting than a pre-release, but Mary would put things right. As she poured herself some water from the bottle on the table, she imagined she was in that car again, looking at a killer, and not in a Portakabin, looking at a smile.

Mary had ensured she'd chair the meeting and went about it efficiently. 'Before we introduce ourselves, I want to remind everyone that this is a pre-release meeting for Mr Macdowall.' She deliberately said Mr, hoping he'd correct her with 'Hmm, hmm, it's *Dr*'.

Instead, he said: 'Liam's fine.'

He murdered his wife. Remember the car, remember he got out. 'This meeting is not about the release of your book. This meeting's about how to manage the likely risk you present to the community. With very high-risk offenders like you, Liam, it's my job to imagine the worst case scenario, and to work backwards to make sure it never happens.'

'And that is?' The lawyer wore a purple, velvet designer jacket with gold trim, a red-and-orange checked tie, pink Argyll socks and fabulous brown cowboy boots. A clever distraction Mary would never fall for.

'That Mr Macdowall murders another woman he's close to.' That shut him up, the dick; she'd ask him where he got the boots after. 'To get things going, as you can see in my home background report, I don't approve of your proposed address. You can't live back at the family house, with your daughter.'

'Such bullshit,' Holly said.

Liam reached over and pressed a calming hand onto his daughter's, but she was furious. 'I told you when you visited for that report that I am not at risk. You think Dad'll hurt me? I saw what Mum did to him, I was there all those years.' Holly held up the report and addressed the rest of them. 'Do you know what she said to me when she visited for this "assessment"? She said: "Your dad's a dangerous misogynist, he hates women so much he kills them. Get him out of your life."'

Mary might have pulled the girl up on her inaccurate quotations if she hadn't had the gist spot on. But what exactly *had* she said at the home visit? She couldn't remember. The girl must have made her overheat, and it was happening again now.

'I put in a complaint about her,' Holly continued. 'I did some digging and apparently she's about to be sacked; that right, Mary? For cheating the system. She told me she's sick of jargon and trickery, tired of trying to help men who should be locked up.' Holly tossed her copy of the home background report on the table. 'So much for rehabilitation. Can't we take this back to the parole board? Surely a feral feminazi social worker should not have this kind of power.'

Many responses raced through Mary's brain: like the list of letters that followed her name. Few folk understood why someone who'd completed a degree in law would choose to be a social worker, but Mary could give a good answer: by accident – her Higher results made her do it. One semester in, though, she realised she wouldn't feel good about herself as a defence lawyer, and that she was not capable of bowing to men in wigs.

Mary had been in more difficult meetings than this, and Holly was right, she didn't give a damn anymore. A twenty-six-year-old with daddy issues wouldn't scare her. She handed another pile of complaint forms to the girl. 'I'd fill in another one if I were you. You think I'm incompetent, you should check out head office. Ask the lawyer, Holly; he's sitting right there with legal advice inside his bright head just waiting to get out. What say you and your qualifications, Mr Harding? Do I have this kind of power? Should Liam appeal my decision about the address?'

Lawyer man whispered to Liam, who whispered to Holly,

and their defeated expressions prompted Mary to continue. 'I was saying that I don't approve of you living with your daughter, Liam, because you murdered a known adult female and the risk assessments conclude it is highly likely that you will be violent to a woman you are close to or intimate with if a few factors come together the way they did ten years ago. The risk factors are all explained in the parole report.'

'Factors like Mum fucking about?' Holly scowled. 'I told you she was screwing around for ages. She was on other affair websites, you know, not just Eat.It.Too. She treated him like shit. I saw her hit him over the head with an egg whisk, but whoever talks about that? Did they think to mention that in court? No, because Dad wanted to protect her memory.'

Her dad intervened. 'It was a pestle, hon.'

'A pestle?' Mary couldn't stop herself saying. 'I hear those things can really mangle your peppercorn.'

Macdowall ignored her; probably sensible. 'I have a backup plan housing-wise.'

The labels were piling up around this Liam Macdowall: entitled, manipulative. *Eyes.*

'And what would that be?'

'A private furnished let in Shawlands. I can give you all the details. It's a well-managed flat in a secure close, and there are no "known adult females" in it.'

Thank God she'd only have to supervise the guy for a few weeks. She wouldn't tell him that yet, though, not until a new worker was allocated, which probably wouldn't happen before she left.

Mary gave everyone a couple of minutes to talk about their role or concerns. When it was Holly's turn, her anger dwindled, and she became tearful. Holly felt terrible that the house was now hers, and that he was not allowed to live in it.

Liam calmed her. 'You have a lot to work through your-self, honey, and I won't be far away.'

What a stunning mess of a girl. She mangled Mary's head. 'If things go well, I might approve the address for an over-night now and then, but that's a way off. Now, before we wrap up, is there anything you'd like to say, Liam?' Mary felt certain he'd have something prepared. He was a showman, her life licensee.

Liam slumped his shoulders so that he'd look smaller and began: 'I want to do everything possible to be no risk. I'm going to abstain from alcohol altogether – shouldn't be too hard after ten years without, but I've asked Tracy to breathalyse me each week. Isn't that right, Tracy? And I'm managing my antidepressants very well; have done for ten years. I will not be coming off sertraline, ever. I want to make good decisions and I'm at your command. I want your help.' Encouraged by the positive vibes from his audience, Liam straightened his shoulders again.

Mary took back control by summarising her powers: 'I must approve your address. I must know where you're working and when. I will visit you at home – announced and unannounced – and you will attend my office weekly to check in and tell me what you've been doing and who you've been seeing. I want to know about any potential rela-tionships before they get intimate, and you should know that I may disclose your offence to that person if you don't. I need to know if you have any intentional contact with children, and if you do, an assessment will need to be made by my childcare colleagues. You can't go anywhere overnight without my approval. I will undertake structured domestic-abuse sessions with you called "What Were You Thinking?" on an individual basis in the office. You will abstain from alcohol and attend counselling weekly, where you will be breathalysed. I will liaise with Tracy regarding the results. I'll check in with your GP about your mental health and medication management. We'll review the licence every three months, see how things are going, if anything needs to change. Failure to comply with any of the above, or with any reasonable instructions I give you in order to promote your rehabilitation and protect public safety, can result in your immediate recall to prison. Get it, Liam?'

'Got it, Mrs Shields.'

Ms. One syllable. Like Miss. Simpler than Missus, by a factor of one. Not difficult at all unless you are a complete fuckwit. And breathe. 'It's *Ms* Shields.'

'*Mzzz* Shields,' Alt-right Derek piped up. 'If Liam meets a girl in a bar he has to ring you before taking her home?'

She knew this instruction would cause problems, might even be newsworthy. She didn't give a shit. 'That sounds like a good idea.'

'You're wanting Liam to check in with you before he has sexual relations?' Derek said. 'How many hours before the first kiss: twenty-four, seven? Three seconds? Or is it before second base, if he's about to touch a breast?' Everyone but Mary laughed. 'Takes the romance out of it, doesn't it?'

'Murdering your wife can do that,' Mary said.

Holly stood, which was not allowed. 'Excuse me! Excuse me! Anyone else think this woman is FUCKED IN THE HEAD?'

The prisoner, the lawyer and the alcohol counsellor walked into a bar. No, they didn't. They stared at Holly, so out of place here with her symmetrical face and use of capitals.

Everyone froze, unsure how to respond.

Except Mary. 'Sit down, Holly. Listen, if I have to breach

you, Liam, you'll get a chance to argue your case with the board, as will I. But it's not what I want. I want you to be law-abiding and happy.' It was half true.

Holly sat down eventually but tried to make it look like her decision.

They were all raging. Must be awful, being told what to do by an idiot social worker.

'But why are you talking about children?' Derek said. 'Why would your colleagues have to get involved if there is a child? Liam's not a paedophile!'

Mary was bored with the constant nit-pickery and conflict. Every day she had to make up scenarios and make up protective restrictions and then make up answers like this: 'Mr McLaverty, if you met someone online, say, then had a date or two, introduced him or her to your kids, and you all really have a nice time, you think this is gonna go somewhere, and it does, and you start falling in love with him or her as much as the children are. Then you find out the new love of your life killed his or her spouse. I wouldn't like that. Social workers wouldn't like that. They'd want you to have all the information you need to ensure the safety of your children. Shall we move on?' She hoped no-one could see the sweat dripping down her chest.

Holly and the lawyer had all crossed their arms but not as tightly as Derek.

Liam was the only one still maintaining composure. 'If happiness seems imminent, you'll be the first to know.'

It'd be quite easy to pounce across the table and stab him in the eye.

And breathe.

'Okay.' Mary exhaled. 'So as long as I've checked out and approved the Shawlands flat, you'll be released on life licence this Friday, so I'll see you at twelve noon, Friday, Kenneth House, 10 Grange Road.'

Derek had turned to page one of his hefty PR itinerary. 'But Liam's doing an interview.'

Mary opened the document. The 2.00 p.m. radio programme was the first of about ten events happening every day over the next month. She closed the itinerary and the meeting.

'Ask for me at reception.'

When she got home, Mary gifted Roddie a Skype-gasm. He was obviously behaving himself – all she needed to do was show him her boobs, the only part of her body that had improved in recent months.

It was only 9.00 p.m. when Mary settled into bed with her laptop and a book. She Googled the novel's title – *Cuck* – and was surprised to discover a world of porn hitherto outwith her radar, an author pic of Liam Macdowall in the mix. She raced to the kitchen for some mega-fresh AAA batteries.

This might well have been the day, the hour, the minute, the moment, that she made the decision that ruined her life. She opened the book at 'Letter Nineteen', which she had read several times already, switched on her bunny, and set the consequences in motion, chanting out loud as she reread: *I must not think about that, I must not think about that.*

2

CUCK, by Dr Liam Macdowall

The Nineteenth Letter

Dearest Bella,
Rab is masturbating in the bottom bunk. I believe he prefers to do it when I am lying above him. I am trying hard to distract myself, hence another letter to you.

I feared prison before I was sentenced, but I don't anymore. I made an excellent decision on day one, which gave me immediate status and has kept me safe. I beat up a paedophile. I knew coming in how I would be treated here – a woman killer, and with money too, not that I have that anymore. I was sitting in line at the health centre when two officers began questioning the man beside me, rather loudly I must say. There is no privacy in prison. The first officer asked him if he felt like killing himself, and it surprised me that he answered honestly. The other officer asked if he had made a plan, which was also a yes.

'No wonder,' said the first officer, 'after what you did, you paedophile prick.'

I was next in line, because I too would have liked to kill myself at that time, and word had somehow got out. The officers went into the office and closed the door, leaving me alone with the beast, and I took the opportunity to crack his clavicle. He fought only with paedo tears, even when I moved his jaw an inch left with my prison-issue trainer. Staff members took their time to intervene. It was a defining moment, Bella, the first time in my mature life that I'd been violent, and the best decision I ever made.

God, no, it was the second time. Obviously. It's amazing how little I still know myself, after three years working on it in here. Amazing. Beating the beast was the second time I had been violent as an adult. The first was when I killed you.

The upshot is that Rab is scared of me. Will he ever finish? He needs a better memory. I almost feel I should give him mine, which is of you, Bella, the first time I saw you. Student Union, 2.00 a.m., intoxicated and dancing to 'Rasputin'. Your outstretched arms made your little dress head to the skies, and I saw your pants and for some reason had to tell you immediately. 'I've seen your pants,' I whispered, and you giggled and kept dancing. I leaned in to breathe on you: 'We have to kiss, you have no choice.'

You liked my tattoos, I know you did. And my accent – same as yours but poorer. And my dancing, which, as you know, is excellent, me swinging you about as if you weighed nothing. You liked the working-class lad made good, my overpowering audaciousness.

'Because if we don't kiss immediately…' I placed your hand on my chest '…I will set off the device that is wrapped around my chest, underneath this shirt. Can you feel it?' Risky strategy, I know. You told me later that even though you couldn't feel anything under my shirt, you should have run for your life rather than kiss me.

I wish you had.

I'm afraid Rab and I climaxed at the same moment. I do hope it's not because I made noises thinking about you, but, Belle, how can I be quiet when I think about you? My regret is noisy, my grief is noisy, my desire for you is noisy.

3

Mary closed chapter nineteen, threw the book on the floor, and messaged Roddie:

—*I just fantasised about a client for the first time ever. I need to leave that fucking job.*

—*I shoulda reciprocated earlier, soz. The author guy?*

—*The wife-killer guy.*

—*Well he could do it for me, too. Look at that pretty face in amongst all those naked threesomes.*

—*You're Googling him?*

—*I Googled 'cuck'.*

Roddie copied and pasted:

—*cuckold, (kuck-uhld), noun: the husband of an adulteress, often regarded as an object of derision. Online, particularly 4chan, the term is used to insult a man who is considered to have 'sold out' or who sacrifices his dignity for female approval.*

—*Hon, don't beat yourself up over him ... ever again. Shall I send you a cock pic?*

Mary gave it some thought.

—*That'd be lovely, thank you xxx.*

It was ten past twelve, Friday, and Liam Macdowall was a no-show. Mary dialled the governor of Lowfield on her ancient work-issue Blackberry.

'Tell me you changed your mind, K. You're keeping him in?'

The governor wasn't usually on first-name bases with social workers, let alone first-letter, but Karen and Mary went way back to the glory days, when terrorists had luxury wings and better food, and when sex offenders wore sex offender-coloured polo shirts. K and Mary had met ten years before in the staff gym, when overweight K was thrown from her runaway treadmill. The unfortunate incident had been on replay in security ever since. And ever since, Mary and Karen had attended the pub on Fridays.

'Nup, he's your problem now,' Karen said. 'But he's been waylaid by a flock of adoring misogynists and some loud lesbians.'

'Any cute ones?'

'Not a one. You in the Toyota shite-mobile? I'll make sure you get through to the G4S entrance, and we'll get you to him, then head off left, not the motorway. Get him out of here.'

Police cars and media vans filled the Lowfield driveway. An officer spotted Mary's car, which was stuck halfway along, and cleared the way through to the G4S entrance, which was beside the steps to the main door. To the left of the steps was a group of women, and a few skinny men, yelling, 'Women hold up half the sky, Women hold up half the sky.' Mary had never heard that expression before and she wondered why her arms weren't better toned if it was so. The women's banners read: *Cuck off*; *Infidelity is not an excuse for murder*; *Domestic Violence IS about gender*; and *Stop the slaughter*.

On the other side of the entrance were the men – about forty of them – holding placards:

Men need protection from abusive wives; 90% of suicides are men and *You want gender equality? Good, I don't want to pay, I don't want to open doors, I don't want to go to war, I don't want to die to save you.*

Mary should have realised sooner, she supposed, but Dr Liam Macdowall – his face, his words, his experience – was the perfect eye for a long brewing storm.

'Men against violence.' One man echoed the words he held. He, like most of the men, wore a black t-shirt with the letter C printed on it in bright red – a nod to Nathaniel Hawthorne's *The Scarlet Letter*. At the front, also wearing scarlet letters, were Derek and Holly.

And there he was, coming through the revolving glass door, stopping on the top step, HMP Lowfield's loud lettering above. The cameras rolled, and Liam Macdowall declared over the mic: 'The first step towards any positive change is to admit you have a problem. My name is Liam Macdowall and I am a pathetic excuse for a man. I'm so pathetic my wife cuckolded me. I am a cuck.' Liam took a t-shirt from Derek and put it over the tight designer one he had on. It looked great. 'The second step is to own it and move on. I wear this C proudly, it is no longer a symbol of my past weaknesses, but an affirmation of my courage.'

The men chanted, 'Courage. Courage. Courage.' The women and vegetarian men booed. Holly burst into tears, hacked her way through the crowd, ran up the stairs and hugged her father. He cried too. Their smiles seemed real when they turned to face the cameras, and faded when Mary barged through to drag them away.

'Are you crazy, Liam? Hide your face, Holly. Quick, follow me.'

The three of them shuffled off towards the car to shouts

about holding up skies, and counter-shouts about being human beings too, which sounded better when the Elephant Man said it.

The two tribes followed them as Mary crawled along the drive. And as they crawled, the synchronised chanting turned into a vicious shouting match.

'You're a cunt,' said one of the women.

'You're too ugly to rape,' said one of the men.

Twenty-five years in the job and the most important lesson Mary had ever learned was that you get more info out of folk if you're driving with them. Hence, Mary had spent as much of every day as possible driving her clients *aboot*. She'd driven schedule-one offenders from prisons to their nice new homes opposite primary schools; ten-year-old kids from their really fucking shite homes to their new really fucking shite homes; and heroin users to rehab, then back to Renfield to get gear. It made people relax, sitting in a car and not having to look at you, and Mary aimed to make the most of that now.

'Holly doesn't think you're a violent man, Liam, even though you murdered her mother.'

'Jesus Christ, see what I mean about her?' Holly said from the back.

'It's okay, Holl.' A tiny vein on Liam's forehead twitched. He paused and turned to Holly. 'She just wants you to be safe, and you are.'

'Bet you say that to all the girls.' Mary wondered if she'd said this out loud, but recently, whenever she'd wondered this and investigated the matter, she invariably had always said the thing she hoped she hadn't. Luckily, this time she felt confident she'd kept some thoughts to herself; like *arsehole*.

Mary pressed *answer* instead of *decline* when her personal mobile rang. Shit.

'Mum?'

She almost hit the car in front of her trying to press *end*. The button wasn't working. Her finger was too sweaty. 'Jack, can I call you back?'

'Where's my charger?' he said.

'Um … can I call you back?'

'It was in my bag when I was at yours last. Did you take it out? Will you stop stealing my fucking stuff?'

Mary checked the rear-view mirror to confirm that Holly was smirking. She wiped her fingers on her jeans, pressed *end*; still too sweaty. 'I'll look at home and bring it over if I find it. Gotta—'

'Never mind, I'll go buy one. Guess what I'm reading?'

To Mary's horror, her son began reciting from *Cuck*. '"Your upper lip is gathered so tightly it's turned an inhuman shade of green." He's flowery, your wife killer!'

Mary finally managed to hang up.

Liam smiled. 'He sounds like an only child.'

Mary had been caught out behaving like a human, as well as breaching confidentiality. She had lost all her power. It took her two deep breaths before deciding to answer. 'He is.'

'Is he cute?' Holly said from the back.

Mary took her eyes off the road to say: 'He's cross-eyed, pock-marked, obese and bald.'

But Holly was looking at Mary's screensaver, and Jack was none of the above.

CUCK, Dr Liam Macdowall

The Thirtieth Letter

Dear Bella,
Derek suggested I record a memory. This is my memory of the first time.

Your upper lip is gathered so tightly it's turned an inhuman shade of green. The cup in your hand is filled with hot tea and has World's Best Mum *written on it. The light in the bathroom is still not working, and there are many other things I've not done, or done but badly, since seeing you last, and you're telling me all of them, over and over, louder and louder, and my non-reaction, you tell me later, is why you throw the mug at me, hot tea and all, and I'm just standing there, like an ice man. I don't stab you with the largest, jagged piece of cup, which now reads only* World's Best. *I don't yell or beg or dial 999 or run to the neighbours for help. What I do, I take one breath, then another, then I say I am taking time out. I do the sign for it, I'm taking time out, and you shout at me until I shut the door and breathe, and breathe, and walk alone. Well, not alone now because of you. The shame you have just started to poison me with: we take our first walk, she and I.*

'Inhuman shade of green', the wanker. His key was under a pot on the landing. Liam unlocked the front door, and seemed as surprised as Mary that Derek McLaverty was already inside. The living area looked like *Cuck* HQ, with books and flyers and t-shirts piled on the floor. Derek and his silver MacBook had made a desk of the dining table. He didn't look Mary in the eye once, and she realised he hadn't since they'd met. He'd called *The Culture Show* and the interview could be done in time if it was over the phone. Did Liam need some water? Anything? He'd be on in five. Mary was as impressed as she was powerless. She scolded herself for the former as she gave Liam his next appointment (Tuesday between 9.00 and 10.00 a.m. Mary was at her best between 9.00 and 10.00 on Tuesdays) and took the number of the mobile phone Derek had bought for him.

In her car, she started the engine and shook her head to reaffirm that she would not listen to Radio Scotland, no way. She put the blinker on. Then she put the radio on:

'*…whose debut novel,* Cuck: Letters to My Dead Wife, *is causing something of a stir among feminist groups and men's rights activists. Fresh from B hall in Lowfield, released just this morning, we have Dr Liam Macdowall. Welcome, welcome to the world. Before at least one of our other guests lays into you, let's start nice: what's it like, the world, after ten years in prison?'*

'*Thanks for having me, Brenda … The world? It feels … unsafe. This morning the lights went on at seven and I shuffled downstairs and stood in line for my tray of breakfast, which was*

*scrambled egg and bacon, and soggy white toast, and I ate it in
my cell – I won't go on. Life was structured; safe, I know, is an
odd word, but that's what it was inside. It became that way at
the three-year mark.'*

'When you found your tribe?'

The presenter was referring to the letter in his book that
was all about his tribe, how he'd lost his malehood on the
outside, piece by piece, because of the women he was forced
to try and be equal with. In the letter (number eighteen,
Mary reckoned) he concluded that the only place men can
flourish these days is in prison.

'Yes, and myself.'

'Does that mean you'd like to go back to prison?'

'God, no. I intend to flourish on the outside. I intend to help
men flourish and be free.'

Mary turned off the radio. It was 2:07, and she was late for
a joint visit to the World's Best Sex Offender with Detective
Sergeant Minnie Mouse, who she texted as she drove.

Fortunately, Min was running even later.

Mary planned to put in her resignation as soon as Roddie's
contract was finalised, which would be any day now. Eighty
grand he was getting, to be head colour-in-er-er on a graphic
novel series Mary should have heard of. Roddie was going to
give her a break, just in the nick of time. The two of them
were going to live the life.

After the flexi incident, Mary had let her boss, Catherine,
know that she intended to leave as soon as possible, and
asked if she could have daily supervision. She hadn't felt so
unable to control her mood since she'd first got her period.

And she was *so* over the job; certain things were pressing her buttons. There was talk of the service being decentralised again, for example. Mary had been centralised and decentralised to fuck, and simply could not handle it happening all over again. Then there was the computer system, SWID, which was soon to be replaced by something that'd take Mary seven years to learn how to use. She had to get out before either of these things happened. In the meantime, she wanted Catherine to be formally aware that she was not feeling herself, and to record the meetings. She had hoped to be sent home to bed, but that was too dangerous for a stage-three girl. Catherine, much younger and much better at everything, also decided it was better not to record Mary's confessions – of which there were many – on the system.

In the last few days, she had handed out eight complaint forms, two of which had been completed and returned to head office. She'd executed the exit of two battered women. She'd made a Sunday roast for an elderly lifer, and told a defence lawyer to fuck off. She'd given two hundred pounds to each of her three lovable rogues, the eighteen to twenty-four-year-olds who carried hammers and kicked heads and the like, but who had a chance of stopping. She'd filled her boot with food, parked at the entrance to the office at lunchtime, and asked clients if they'd like to help themselves. She had also openly promoted the smoking of marijuana to all her colleagues and clients, and had suggested to the governor of Lowfield that it be offered to all inmates in abundance and for free. If she was to undertake an Acute 2007 risk assessment on herself now, she'd score on every item: hostility, sexual preoccupation, rejection of supervision, emotional collapse, collapse of social supports, and substance abuse. In other words, Mary was at very high risk of causing catastrophic harm, and she wanted management to know.

The supervision sessions were at 4.45 p.m. – a sacred time in social work. Even though the office now enjoyed a flexitime system, which Mary had allegedly abused ('Did I sexually assault it?' she'd asked her boss's boss, Shirley, a week ago), everyone wanted out at 4.45 p.m. on the dot, like in the good old pre-flexitime days, when the time of release was certain. After the visit with Minnie Mouse, Mary reported to Catherine and reflected on the errors of judgement she had made since they last met, the first being that she had fantasised about her new client to the point of orgasm. With great lethargy, Catherine noted this and the many other points in the hard-backed red notebook Mary carried in her satchel that bore the title: *IF I CHICKEN OUT, PLEASE USE THIS TO SACK ME*, then said: 'You should go to his launch tonight.'

'Did you not listen to my masturbation story?'

Catherine read out loud as she added another misdemeanour to the notebook: '*Attended handsome ladykiller's work-related event, clearly breaking professional boundaries.*'

'Take someone with you, but I agree with you about this guy, Mary. Where on the risk assessment do we score the item "sudden fame"? Right now, in my opinion, Macdowall's risk is through the roof. Go to the launch.'

Catherine shut the book and handed it back to Mary. 'It is so *fun* having a rogue worker! But no more than two drinks, don't go to the afterparty, and if you don't put in your resignation as promised I will take you on a day trip to Argyle, and on the way back I will drive you into a river and watch you drown.'

'That is *so* fucked up.'

'Go to the book launch, and keep an eye on him and his cronies. It's ten past five! Get out of here. Go.'

Jack turned up at six to look for his charger. He was such a tight-arse. Mary had no idea where he got it from, as she and Roddie loved nothing more than to throw money away. Like most Glaswegians, Jack had lived at home while studying for his degree, leaving only when he was offered a semi-job with a law firm. Two months earlier he and his seven-year-old Labrador, Marty, had moved out. He was kickass at the job, Mary's mate Adeela had heard, had a great career ahead of him. He was a kickass man.

'Told ya.' Jack's charger was plugged in beside Mary's bed. He embraced succinctness ten years ago and hadn't said a word more than necessary since.

'Sorry.' She didn't mean it. She paid for the fucking thing. And she could do with a few more words now and then. To provoke him, Mary showed him the practice comedy set she was working on.

'I hate it. And it's *so* 2017. Oh my God, turn it off, bin it, never show that to anyone ever.'

It was too late. And too good. She'd already emailed her #metoo video to her teacher, Fi, ahead of this week's heckling class. Her sets in class had been stiff and safe, and Fi had set her the homework of being free and bold and outrageous and honest, and to film herself at home performing. Jack's response encouraged her. Comedy was supposed to be uncomfortable.

This night class was one of the many risky things Mary was doing to avoid her now-empty nest. Stand-up on Thursdays, yoga Tuesdays, water-colour painting Saturday afternoons (she never went, but she'd written it in her diary in red pen every Saturday for the next six months, which was a damned fine start). She was considering choir too, because the truth was Mary's voice was haunting. She'd always known it and over the years a few had confirmed it, so choir was going to be either Mondays or Sundays. Life was busy. Life was good. Life would be great.

Before heading out, Mary messaged Roddie on Facebook:

—*Off to see Misogyny Man. Have fun in Cairns, but don't swim in any body of water or you'll die. In fact, stay inside the hotel, will you?*

—*No, but if I go out I promise to take the first-aid kit you gave me.*

It weighed two kilos. Mary had heard terrible things about Australia.

—*Watch out for my editor – Rich from RG Books. Say hi from me.*

A kiss and a smiley face later, and fifty-two-year-old mum set off to town with twenty-four-year-old son.

The crowd outside Waterstones was exactly the same as the one at Lowfield that morning. Mary wondered if they might even have shared the same transport: *Anti-feminists to the left, feminists to the right, or if it suits your definition of yourself to sit in the aisle or perhaps to lie in the luggage rail, go ahead.* Mary bet if someone started singing 'The Back of the Bus They Cannae Sing', everyone would've joined in till they arrived at Next Altercation.

She intended to part ways with Jack in Argyll Street, but

he was hovering at the bookshop window, which was filled with *Cuck* posters. 'You can't come in.'

She shouldn't have said this. It caused him to go in. Jack spotted free wine and grabbed two cups, nudging his way to the front as Macdowall began reading the second letter he wrote to his dead wife.

6

CUCK, Dr Liam Macdowall

The Second Letter

Dear Bella,
As a result of the Eat-It-Too hacking, two people are known to
have committed suicide. One man, Massimo Quadrelli, hurled
himself off a bridge, got his foot caught in a railing and dangled
there for ten minutes before his Nike gave way. I wonder if
Massimo changed his mind as he swung wildly in the wind,
if he forgave his wife for breaking her vows and was clawing
upwards when the shoelace broke. A friend of Colin McTighe
lost his business. It's been The War of the Roses in that house:
the social has gone in. In hundreds of families, addictions and
depressions have taken hold, and in ours, you died. The blast
radius of that hacking is still growing, it will for years, for gen-
erations. It has increased in size since my first words in this letter
to you, 'Dear Bella', only moments ago. There is a good chance
that since I began writing, someone has poured a drink and it
is morning time where they live; there is a very good chance a
child is crying because Mummy put Daddy in jail, and the odds
are high that someone is making a better plan than Massimo
Quadrelli. Three years ago today, at 9.00 p.m., three thousand
names and addresses were published online – three thousand
from all over the world. Yours – Isabelle Duff, 24 Harris Place,
Glasgow – was just one of them, and look at the damage that

caused. Imagine, Bella, imagine if the other two thousand nine hundred and ninety-nine have, or are to be, as harmed as us.

I am just back from counselling with Julie, and we have both concluded that I was not authentic with you. After our first dance at the Union we walked to your flat because there was no way I was going to take you to mine, and I was already pretending to be all sorts of things I wasn't. It is hard once you've misrepresented yourself. You find you must take the next step to prove to yourself that you've not really told a lie. Perhaps you do like Cezanne and kitesurfing, you think. Why wouldn't you like those things? I pretended I liked James Taylor, and because of one of many momentary teenage misrepresentations I had to listen to him in the car, in the kitchen, and in our bedroom for a decade because I didn't want to admit that the man you fell in love with does not exist.

Back to our first date: we were walking along Dumbarton Road and you turned your attention to a billboard that offended you – washing powder, I think it was. I pretended to care, and I didn't. I was seventeen and I liked breasts, yours in particular at that moment, which is why I went further than pretending to care, referencing several sexist advertisements that were outrageous and should be banned.

I kept that up for years, Bella. Just as you pretended you didn't mind me earning less than you, like you didn't mind being with a man who put up shelves that fell down again, a man who sometimes wanted a woman to make the first move, a man who sometimes couldn't get it up, or couldn't come, who liked pornography, like every other man. I've talked to dozens of men in here, and we all feel the same: we had lost our pack out there, believed it a mythical thing, but it is real. We have been hiding in here, thriving in here, all this time. Outside we all feel like nothing – liars, pretending liars. But it's changing, we will not pretend anymore, we are coming out. I hate James Taylor, Bella. I love advertisements with breasts in them, I love pornography and I love you.

7

Macdowall had performed with such emotion and strength that his talent appeared Shakespearean. The audience throbbed towards explosion. What a bunch of idiots, Mary thought, before she noticed that Holly was standing shoulder to shoulder with her son, who had a look of rapture on his face and was clapping as hard as he possibly could. She caught Holly's eye, her finger doing the talking for her: *You. Get away. From him.*

Holly gestured back with her finger: *You,* then with two: *Get fucked.*

One day she'd have to kick that girl's head in.

Jack and Holly seemed to be breaking the rules of personal space, which made Mary tip a last drop from her plastic cup. Jack was a feminist. Why wouldn't he be? He had no business flirting with a girl like Holly. He cooked, cleaned, did his own washing, liked his mother as much as he liked his father – maybe a little less, but everyone liked Mary a little less than Roddie, especially recently. She even had proof on Tinder that Jack was a feminist. A girl had asked him and he'd said, 'Of course.'

Right now, his right side was touching Holly's left side. The vixen whispered something that made him giggle, then she looked over his shoulder to smirk at Mary. Mary grabbed Jack's arm and dragged him a few people away.

'Any questions?' Liam asked. 'The young lady in blue! Can you get the mic to the lady? Thanks.'

'Dr Macdowall, why do you think your book is so controversial?' asked the lady in blue.

At the same time, Mary was whispering a question of her own: 'Why did you clap?'

Jack had obviously decided no words were necessary at this juncture.

Mary repeated the question. 'Why would you clap at him?'

'Why not?'

'He killed his wife.' Mary had whispered this a little loudly.

When the crowd's attention returned to Macdowall, Jack replied, 'You're an arsehole, Mum. I'm going.'

'Please. Please do.' Mary may have pushed him a smidgeon. She really wanted him to go. She did not, however, want Holly Macdowall to follow him.

Macdowall took his jacket off, flung it on the chair and talked to the audience as if he was cooking for them at home. Mary would have a think about how he did that and try it out in stand-up class.

'Because I'm a murderer,' Liam answered the lady in blue.

'It's cos you're gorgeous!' someone screeched from the back, causing a ripple of giggles and camera flashes.

'My love for you is noisy, Liam!' another yelled, and everyone laughed.

'Well, thank you.' He shifted attention to the woman who'd asked the first question. 'What's your name?'

'Melanie.'

'I think it's striking a chord, Melanie, because…' Liam leaned his bum against the lectern. He owned that stage; had to give him that. 'I have been defined by one act, one minute of my life. For the other hundreds and thousands

– millions – of minutes, I wasn't killing my wife.' He nodded to Mary; he'd obviously heard her earlier. The book fills in the minutes, makes me real, questions your view of what a murderer is, but perhaps more importantly, it changes your perception of what a man is.'

Mary failed to draw upon the decision-making skills she'd drummed into two thousand plus clients and grabbed the roaming microphone. 'Is that wine you're drinking?'

Macdowall put his red-filled cup on the table behind him. 'This is Mary Shields, everyone. My parole officer!' The audience roared with laughter. Macdowall waited the right amount of time before picking up a bottle of water and twisting the cap. 'She is damn good at her job, ladies and gentlemen. Did you see that?' Liam tipped his Evian at Mary and took a sip.

When Mary got to the front of the signing queue, Macdowall grabbed a fresh copy of the book from his pile and poised his pen. 'Shall I make it out to Mary or Mzzzz Shields?'

'I don't want a book, thanks. I waited to tell you you'll be getting a first formal warning, for drinking.'

Liam leaned in. 'Did you see me drink wine from the cup? It's on the table over there if you'd like to get it to forensics.'

Mary was very competitive when it came to holding silences.

'It's a bit stalkery, coming to my book launch, is it not?' he said.

'I get paid to stalk you, by the Scottish Office.' Two girl fans in the line behind Mary began giggling. 'You're very popular with idiot women.'

'That's not a very sisterly thing to say.' Somehow, Macdowall was now signing a book, which he handed to her. She glanced at the *Dear Mary* inscription inside and slammed the hardcover shut.

'Now I'm gonna have to pay for that.' She walked over to the table, lifted Liam's plastic cup, smelt it, wrapped it in a tissue, and put it in her bag, returning to Liam's table to interrupt the next in line. 'You'll get the warning letter Tuesday at nine.'

She only dared to look at the inscription once she was back in her car.

> *To Mary,*
> *Who's not an idiot,*
> *Unfortunately,*
> *Liam xx*

8

Hurtling towards Renfield, Mary organised her thoughts. Her first appointment of the day was Macdowall. She had to give him a written warning, lay down the law, do a ten-minute check-in, and explain the What Were You Thinking? domestic abuse work she was supposed to start straight away. All good, she'd get to Lowfield by eleven, no bother. Shit, was the indecent images cretin at eleven? Mary groped for her diary as she drove and glanced at a messy and over-filled Tuesday. She'd booked the prison interview for ten, which meant she'd have to be done with Macdowall by 9.15 a.m., which meant she had fifteen minutes for all the above. Fifteen minutes, she thought to herself as she draped her ID round her neck and shut the car door. Plenty of time.

Flex Machine says: minus one minute. Yet again, the hours she'd accrued last month had been wiped. Thank God she was leaving. She'd head-butt the machine otherwise.

Prior to 9.00 a.m., Mary managed the usual conversation with Lil.

'Ten, one. What are you?'

'Nine, twelve. Down another two,' Mary said.

'That's the crazy eating the calories.'

'I think it is the crazy.'

'Made the GP appointment yet?'

If Mary ever had the misfortune of being social worked, she would want to be social worked by Lil. 'I will.'

'You promise?' Lil held out her pinkie.

Mary promised.

Five to nine. She typed and printed the formal warning, located and copied the items she needed for the session and Googled Derek McLaverty's latest movements. It seemed to Mary that Derek was Liam's significant other, and that she would have to find a way to work with him or she would fail.

In the last twenty-four hours, Derek had been very active on his public Facebook page:

'MEN:
Do not be sorry for being a man
There is no guilt in being born male.
They are telling us otherwise but we must not apologise.'

Mary scrolled down Derek's timeline:
'I've been told extreme views are okay because they have to make up for past injustices. Present and future injustice is as wrong as past. Possibly more as it is so consciously done.'

In the last week, Derek McLaverty had been to HMP Lowfield; then to see his lawyer about Nel, twenty-two, freshly qualified and – at this moment – hyperventilating at her Pod-2 desk.

According to Nel's profile notes, Derek had failed to attend supervised contact seven times in a row, upsetting and unsettling his wee boys week after week. Nel was about to give up on pursuing Derek for contact, focusing instead on the safety of mother and sons. In the most recent case note, Nel requested the case be transferred due to verbal abuse.

She had also placed a red flag against Derek's name.

Derek's online commentary in relation to Nel was all about inexperience and appearance. Poor Nel. 'I refuse to have that slag watch me play with my kids,' he blogged. 'What does she know about parenting?'

Mary raced over to Nel's desk and started a conversation, social-work-style: 'Derek McLaverty.'

It was all she needed to say; the name inspired terror. 'Isn't he inside?'

Mary had ruined the girl's day, as he was not inside, not at the moment anyway.

'I can't chat,' said Nel. 'Got a hearing. But watch the guy. Small-man syndrome.'

'Or just bad-man syndrome?'

'Bit of both. The guy who's always getting chucked, y'know? The guy scratching his eczema and yelling at girls online from his smelly bedroom. He's back living with his parents in the Mearns now, ha! With his mummy and daddy, and I'm not sure they like him much either. Watch out for him. He hates social workers *so* much. I'm ruining his life, see. Me and Pam. One more incident and we'll be denying him all contact. He won't see his kids again.'

'No?'

'I'll send you some incident reports.'

'Cheers, Nel. Good luck with the hearing.'

Back at her desk, Mary continued what she now realised was the first step in a risk assessment on Derek McLaverty – the gathering of information. He had created a Cuck page (which Mary followed), its profile picture the cover of Macdowall's book. He'd tagged author Dr Liam Macdowall in the eighty photos he'd taken of the launch, five of which clearly showed her abstinent lifer drinking red wine, all of which were liked by at least ten young women. Groupies, jeez. Victim access was going through the roof.

Liam Macdowall hadn't showed by 9.14 a.m., so Mary ripped up the first formal warning and typed and printed a second formal warning, knowing and not caring that she'd broken another of her work rules: any correspondence written in anger must go through a twenty-four-hour cooling-off period before printing and sending. No time for that: she had to be at Lowfield by ten for … what again? Bradley Clancy; nice name not guy.

She was almost out the door when: 'Mary! Mary!'

Fuck, it was the green-haired student social worker. 'Hi, I'm Hattie,' she'd chirped when they met. 'I identify as cis, so my pronouns are she and her.'

This had made Mary's head hurt, which made her accidentally agree to give Hattie a programme of offence-focused work for her first case: a gambler with autism named Andrew. 'Can you get those worksheets for me today, Mary? Andy's very vuln—'

Mary put her headphones on, but the girl was screeching. Jeez, now she was following her out the door, down the exterior stairs.

'Mary? It's just, he stole from his mum last week and he hates himself. He's having panic attacks. He's in court next week. Mary?'

She made it to her car just in time.

On the way to prison, Mary stopped off in Shawlands, pressed the service buzzer on Macdowall's block and went straight up. When he didn't answer her third knock, she put the (first and) second written warning(s) through his door, pausing momentarily before letting go. It was the right thing to do. In five days, Macdowall had breached almost every condition of his licence. He was dangerous. Two strikes, one to go.

One prison interview, two home visits, three office appointments, and a message from Macdowall later (he'd arrived at reception at the office at 9.16 a.m., late bus, where was she? could she pls call?), and Mary was pouring a kitchen Sangiovese (extra, extra large) and putting on her 'I'm Home!' playlist. One of her dad's faves, 'Rock My Soul in the Bosom of Abraham', compelled her to pour another (which meant she had to empty the first), grab the egg whisk, and sing into the ceiling-to-floor mirror opposite the kitchen window. There were a lot of mirrors in Mary's house – one in each room, at least – but this one was her favourite at this time of day. The immensity of it made her little, and Mary yearned to shop in the petite section. She lifted her shirt and considered her torso: slim yes, but no jutting hip-bones, a thing she'd had once during a very unhappy period and wanted again. She'd stop eating altogether for a bit, up the sit-ups. Yeah.

Empty nest, schmempty nest. Mary could now drink on a Tuesday if she liked, although she'd always liked. She'd already turned some of the hall into a gym; had rented a rowing machine and tried to assemble a gaggle of weights (they were too heavy). With Jack now gone, she could sew Roman blinds in the sewing area, which was now taking up a fifth of his room – maybe she'd do that after she binge-rewatched *Project Runway* and learned how to sew. And then, in between the satisfying sewing of seams, she might choose to meditate using the app she'd downloaded and the mat she got on Amazon and placed under the living-room window. But first: a joint.

After the Afghan Kush her mate Johnny dropped round every Monday – which, for the first time ever, she smoked with the window closed, not at all worried about kids or smell or cancer – Mary opened all the windows in the house, brushed her teeth, and checked the time.

6.05 p.m. Too early to ring Roddie.

Meditation had been stressful for Mary ever since she first tried it two months ago, and she rarely persevered nowadays. She'd been at it only one minute, when the intensity and uselessness of doing nothing but breathing created a current that seemed to Taser her to the mat. Mary acknowledged the shuddering feeling, the tsunami of screams in her chest, the insatiable itch of shins she'd scarred attempting to sate these last months. She acknowledged these terrible feelings, shared them with the universe, and waited for the zzzzzzzzzzzzz to go away like the horny Zen abbot promised it would. (Maybe she'd misunderstood the abbot. Probably, as she'd come up with three comedy sets during class.) She was still Tasered, even after the second joint … or because of it? Mary did not want to answer that question. The notion that wine and weed might also move out of home – just, nup.

Mary bade farewell to the yoga mat – till next time, she namaste-ed – and took head seat at the kitchen table, which had been un-eat-on-able since she'd bought the thousand-piece jigsaw on eBay a week and a half ago. She pondered her progress: she had divided bits of the Cinque Terre into fifteen piles, and she had matched a total of twenty edges. With intense method, Mary subdivided and scanned the pile of edge pieces with sky included – left to right, and back again; left to right and back again. None of them fitted together. There was sky with cloud, sky with less cloud, dark sky, light sky: was that a match? She turned the music four notches above what was socially acceptable to Nora in 1/1, poured a third glass of wine, and slowly moved edge piece with light sky #1 towards edge piece with light sky #2, confident and celebratory that they'd fit together the way she and Roddie did.

Fuck this fucking jigsaw puzzle. It was as impossible as knitting.

Mary changed into the lace teddy she'd bought as a reward for maintaining the five-two diet for five days. She adjusted her cleavature and pose, deciding on and holding her choice, which was sitting on the end of the bed in high-heeled boots, her back straight, tits forwards, chin up and over the fence, and then FaceTimed the man who, twenty-seven years earlier, having just shaken her hand and established her name, leaned in and said: 'Tell me ten things about yourself, Mary Shields.' This opening, and what happened next, meant they had to be together.

'One: I weigh nine stone eight today. Apparently, I had a kebab last night … It's true what Rohypnol victims say: somehow, *not* remembering *is* the worst thing. Two is, I love kebabs. Three, I have no pants on.'

That was all Roddie needed to know. 'The woman I shall marry, everybody!' He tried to lift Mary hunter-gatherer manner, and almost managed to get her off the ground before changing tack. 'Fancy a kebab?'

Mary said I do.

When Roddie answered, she'd say, 'I have no pants on', which wasn't any less true all these years later.

No answer.

Mary topped off the third glass while FaceTiming, phoning, texting, voicemailing and emailing her beloved, who was obviously in bed with a Comic Con groupie. After years as a struggling artist – i.e., one who struggles to make art – Roddie had unexpectedly (to Mary) taken the graphic-novel world by storm with his amazing colouring-in. Today he was being gang-tagged on Facebook by girls with nose piercings, tattoos, cleavages and an apparently genuine interest in comic books.

Half recalling the only Zen class she'd ever done, Mary owned the ugly feeling she had by saying it out loud: 'I am jealous!' and flung her jealousy to the universe, where she'd also recently hurled anger, rage, hatred, self-loathing, hunger, lust, and (last week) a sudden urge to steal a car.

8.35 p.m. What should she do before trying Roddie again? Eat some liquorice allsorts? Mary had bought liquorice allsorts once a month for the last thirty-five years and had only recently realised why: they fed her period monster. As she hadn't had her period monster for some time, there were none in the larder, which was fine because Mary didn't feel like them anyway, apparently because she'd dried up. Liquorice allsorts: another casualty of menopause.

She could eat a Thai green curry, and/or, (probs *and*) some duck spring rolls. There were twelve of those in the freezer. No, no food, not till she'd won Roddie back from his Comic Con groupies with a flat stomach and a willingness to be filthy.

How to fill the time … Bath? Walk? Read? Ring Mum? (She really should ring her mum). Sing? Stand-up practice? Guitar practice? (She should learn a fifth chord.)

Wank!

Each week, Mary scored the sexual preoccupation of her

Nasties, as she called her seven sex offenders. Not to their faces. To their faces she called them Jimmy, Mick, Nick, Robert, Rob, Robert 2 and Michael (Mick 2 if he was being less of an arsehole). Each week she was required to ask them how many times they'd masturbated since she last saw them, and each week the Nasties replied with one of two responses:

1. Never (of which there were the following
    sub-categories):
    a. Five of her seven registered sex offenders said they
        had not managed an erection for decades and
        therefore not since Mary last saw them.
    b. Three of the five of the seven said they hadn't come
        since they committed their unforgivable offence.
    c. Two of the three of the five of the seven said they'd
        injured themselves trying in the past and didn't go
        there for that reason.

Or…

2. Two to three times per week while fantasising about
    consenting adults, like any normal person. (Two of
    the seven told this lie.)

If Mary herself answered the same question honestly, she'd probably be arrested. Masturbating more than three times a week was a red flag, which scored one on the 'acute' risk assessment; not a good score, but not as bad as two. Even with dying ovaries and a parched canal, Mary still wanked daily and was therefore officially sexually preoccupied. Since Jack moved out, the availability and ease of this low-calorie activity surprised and overjoyed her each evening. It was like finding a tub of praline-and-cream Häagen-Dazs in the freezer when you know you did not buy it.

Mary closed the bedroom curtains and took off her lace teddy. Lil said she always walked round her flat naked and that it was great, but Mary just felt cold, and sorry for Lil. She jumped under the duvet, inserted a giant syringe of gel into her fanny to keep her menopausal minge moist, added a tad of KY to the outside and buzzed away at her drowsy clitoris.

Sober, Mary could muster and hold elaborate lady-horn scenes that required minimal manual labour and ended in a grand mal.

After one large glass of red, Mary required a vibrator and absolute silence in order to come.

Two glasses and she needed aggressive equipment as well as reasonably dodgy porn (she found the search term 'reluctant' worked every time).

Three glasses of red wine required a miracle. One time, Mary pretended to herself that she'd climaxed just to get some sleep. But she was determined tonight. It'd make her feel better. Which meant she'd also score a one on the 'sex as coping' 'acute' risk assessment item. Basically, Mary was dangerous and should be locked up – not like Steven Netherhill, who'd filmed and watched his wee girls in the loo for three years but *never* touched himself while alone, he told Mary each week, because that would be dirty. Netherhill liked seeing his kids shitting, though – loved that.

I must not! Every pleasure had become infected by her job. Mary tossed her frustration and her vibrator into the imaginary river, where she'd also thrown something else recently: her jealousy. That was it: her jealousy. Where was Roddie?

Mary put Roddie's boxers and t-shirt on and tried him

again, and again. She poured herself a carefully measured fourth glass (carefully measured = being unable to fit any more alcohol into largest available receptacle, which is why quite a lot of it spilled on the duvet), and put on a sad song for no reason. It wasn't like she decided to listen to a sad song, it wasn't conscious; not like she wanted to be sad. Who'd choose that? She turned on the bath taps, poured half a bottle of bubble bath in, and waited for UK plumbing's best to fill the tub.

Seven minutes later, Mary considered getting in but decided against it. Too many times she'd been impatient – a trait she would address during week one of her newly gained freedom; and too many times she'd got out of the bath even angrier than when she got in.

9.47 p.m., fourth glass un-had, party over. Time to perform a huge number of grooming rituals, such as removing food from broken molars, taking an assortment of vitamins to improve her personality and trimming her nose hairs with the Phillips Precision Trimmer she had pretended to buy for Roddie. Even alone, she could not look as she let the trimmer slip from her nose to her upper lip and chin, gathering downy fluff in its wake and leaving her face silky-smooth and female. In the bathroom mirror (the bathroom *was* a mirror, floor to ceiling) Mary pulled at her cheek with her fingers and counted the seconds it took for her flesh to return to its original position. One … two … three…

FaceTime calling! Mary raced to her laptop in the bedroom. Without donning one of the many pairs of reading glasses dotted around the house, she pressed the button that would make Roddie appear and yelled at a fuzzy screen: 'Are you fucking someone else? Where have you been?'

'Um, Mary?' The voice was deeper than Roddie's.

Mary moved back several feet until Macdowall came into focus. He was calling from the Cuck Facebook page she should never have joined. Idiot. Mary dropped to the floor, out of sight.

'So sorry, I've been ringing you all night,' Macdowall said.

'Well, it's inappropriate to ring me all night,' Mary yelled from ground zero, 'even more so after 10.00 p.m. and on private video.'

'I'm really sorry. I've been trying since eight. I didn't see anything.'

But he was looking at the bed. Shite, the vibrator was on the mattress. Mary reached for the keyboard to turn the video off and looked up at the mess she'd made of the super-king-size mattress she and Roddie turned over every five years. It was stained with red wine and littered with crumpled linen, Just Ears, vaginal gel and syringe, KY, egg whisk, and lace teddy.

'I've been calling and calling your work mobile. The video's off now. It's safe for you to come up.'

Mary did not take his word for it. She crawled into the hall and switched on her work mobile. Twelve missed calls, seven voicemails, three texts. She always turned it off at home.

She shuffled back into the bedroom. 'I told you to call the emergency line out of hours.'

'But, it's very delicate. And urgent. And I believe you're the only person who can give me permission?' Macdowall was slurring his words; he was obviously under the influence. There was music on in the background and a woman was laughing.

'Permission to do what?'

'I've met someone.'

'Lovely.'

'And she's here, at mine. You said I have to get permission … first.'

Mary had haggled for hours with the board over the intimacy clause in Macdowall's life licence. Her boss, Catherine, thought it was worth a shot; and three of four parole-board members agreed, but none of them had thought through the process of permission-giving, which, as usual for social work, was obviously ridiculous.

'Her name's Fiona Bellwood and she's thirty-five. She wants to be a writer. I'll put her on?'

Mary didn't have time to say no; Fiona Bellwood was on the line. 'Hello, Mrs Shields? In the interests of full disclosure, I do have a twelve-year-old son, James, but he's not here, he's with his dad.'

Macdowall laughed in the background. He was probably naked.

'You want to have sex with Macdowall tonight, is that right, Fiona?'

'Yes, I would, if that's okay with you. God, this is weird.'

'I'm sorry, but he doesn't have my permission. We'd need time to do an assessment.' If anyone ever told Mary they'd need time to do an assessment before answering a simple question, she'd slam an empty bottle of red wine over their head.

'So, you're saying?'

'Go home, Fiona.'

'And if I don't?'

Macdowall had grabbed the handset. 'She's going home.' His tone was defeated. Good. 'But I like her. We spent all day together.'

'So get a joint account.'

'Gimme a break. It's been over eleven years. This feels

unreasonable. And the second warning, really, in my very first letter – can you do that: both at once? I came to the office. You'd gone.'

'I left at 9.14 a.m. The appointment was for nine. We can argue about it in front of the board if you like.'

'Okay, no worries. Sorry for calling like this, it won't happen again.'

'Good. And to be clear, the answer to your question is no. Fiona needs to go home. It's late and I'm not being paid, and you must never contact me this way again. It's completely inappropriate. I'll be in touch tomorrow.'

Macdowall barely managed an 'okay' before hanging up, and Mary knew he'd screw Fiona Bellwood anyway. Probably already was. From behind.

In order to not think about that, Mary had a second joint out the window. Laptop in the optimum viewing spot, she then assumed the foetal position in bed, and without seeing which series or episode was loaded (no glasses nearby) pressed 'play'. If Mary had less Catholic guilt (her membership had lapsed, but not its side-effects), she'd spend all day and all night watching *Sex and the City* these days. She'd stumbled on season four – the best, in Mary's opinion – episode seventeen: 'A Vogue Idea'. Mary noticed that the opening music had already changed her breathing. She felt the stories of the day – and the night – floating away. Ahhh, home.

9

CUCK, Dr Liam Macdowall

The Thirty-Seventh Letter

Dear Bella,
Rab just left and I cried. In the end, he was happy for me, he called me 'class', said he was proud to know a man who had made it – a doctor – even if I couldn't help with the vibrant rash he regularly insisted on showing me. It is finally a good thing to hail from Balshagray! It made me think about home, actually. I believe I may have been happy as a child.

I haven't flown solo since I was on remand. For five months back then, I waited alone in a cold, bare cell wearing trainers with no laces. I spent most of those months arguing with my lawyer, a thirty-year-old plain Jane who wanted me to stitch you up, Bella, which I admit I thought about doing. Our daughter even begged me to – she needed a parent, but I couldn't because you mattered more than I did. This, my counsellor, Julie says, is as unhealthy as not being authentic. A healthy relationship, according to the domestic abuse 'work' she programmes into the minds of men like me is: I matter, you matter. *Some of what she says seems logical, but what does it matter?*

Before the trial, my cell shutter opened every fifteen minutes for 140 days. That's 3,360 times. And each of those times, I would have to declare very quickly: 'I'm alive,' as if saying 'present' to Miss Parkitny in primary two. Maybe that's what she was checking back then – 'Anyone dead since yesterday?' Robert Parkitny, her son, was nunchucked to death by David Burns, so the question was fair enough.

I am not being watched these days, and I know I should be careful about what I allow myself to dwell on. I should not think about mattering in the real world, or about the day I killed you, or about us watching Sex and the City.

I was watching it because you always wanted me afterwards. I think it was the episode where Samantha says: 'Women are for friendships. Men are for fucking.' Or was it on the one when Charlotte could not stomach an uncircumcised penis, but her adoring potential beau understood because all other women hated it too, and he asked her if she would wait till he healed, and she said yes. It might have been that one. She waited, and the sex was better without the disgusting skin God had put on it, and the beau loved it so much he dumped her so he could share it around. Yes, it was that episode. You and I had watched the whole thing, start to finish, no loo or kitchen breaks, and then I kissed you. You stiffened and said: 'I don't feel connected with you.' So I made every effort to connect with you, but failed, by which time your need for connection had become mad. I said, 'Fine, forget it,' and had a long bath, which was the exact thing that makes unconnected wives very mad indeed. Holly saw you kick at the bathroom door until your foot bled. If I had called the police or the neighbours, they would have found a small woman with a bleeding foot and a large naked man who could not think of an explanation he would be happy to relay.

10

Mary woke to the opening credits of season six, episode five, and smiled. She was lucky. Her partner loved *Sex and the City*. She stretched, and found she was frowning.

Hey babe, she messaged Roddie. *Out of ten, how much do you love* Sex and the City?

No reply, and she had to get to work.

Home visits were a good way to start a hangover day. Most of Mary's guys would still be asleep at nine-thirty, and kind of sober, and if her incessant knocking managed to rouse them it'd only be for a minute, as they'd be desperate to take whatever to get through the morning. Jimmy McKinley's 1979 and 2017 crimes were the only things worse than his person. It took him a few minutes to Zimmer to the door and, like last week's shorts, Jimmy's Y-fronts failed to cover him. Mary shielded her eyes – 'Go and put your trousers on!' – uncovering them when she heard the bedroom door close, then using the seconds to snoop about. The living room was a shrine to Jimmy's wife, who'd had a stroke the day of his arrest for 'historical incest' – a term that angered Mary. The only incest that wasn't historical was happening right now, and that was historical now too. After they arrested Jimmy, they looked at his PC and he was also done for 'child pornography'. Don't even get Mary started on the term 'child pornography'.

When Mary decided to get her diploma, she believed

it would be her role to stand on bridges and stop people jumping off. Very soon after qualifying she realised she would never stand on bridges. She and everyone else were too busy catching casualties downstream. Except for sex offenders. If you saw a drowning sex offender being swept with the current you threw a large rock at him. Mary had done her best work in her first five years in the job. Those early cases were the ones she could recall, where she'd made the time and had an impact. She should have been forced to resign at the five-year mark. Every worker should.

Jimmy spent most of his life in an armchair surrounded by photos of Hilda, who looked like a burst couch, in Mary's opinion, but Jimmy thought she was wonderful now she was dead, and he cried if you mentioned her name. It's not like Jimmy could've done any better than Huge Hilda: what with his skin condition and relentless child-abusing. A wedding photo balanced precariously on a small table beside his arm-chair, in case the guilt skipped Jimmy's mind for a moment. He was still in his bedroom, so Mary checked his mobile and TV history, yelling through to let him know that's what she was doing. Every week another complex task was added to her job description, the latest being that she had to check the devices of her sex offenders. If she found anything dodgy, or if they'd deleted their search history, she would need to respond in a manner befitting a sudden increase in risk. But in a technology battle against an internet sex offender, Mary knew she'd have no chance of being remotely competent. She couldn't even figure out how to use voicemail on her work-issue Blackberry.

Jimmy and his Zimmer came back into the lounge, wearing the shorts that hadn't hidden his bits last visit. Mary swiped and tapped and nodded and pressed as if she had a

BSc in computer science and a masters in the dark-or-deep net-or-web. With a raised brow, she focused on the first line of Jimmy's only recent Yahoo email, then on the last line, then on the first again, deducing with confidence and out loud that Jimmy should take a meter reading, for npower, by Friday if possible.

To regain power, Mary looked round the room for another device. She didn't even need a warrant, fucker. She spotted a black plastic box with holes and shit in it beneath the radiator. 'Pass me that please, Jimmy.'

Apparently, it was a blow heater. 'These are expensive, are they not? You should get a combi boiler system. There are grants, I think.'

Jimmy nodded as if to say: *Indeed, I am guilty of tossing my PIP money to the wind.* Then he put the non-device extravagance back in its creepy little place beneath the radiator.

'I'm putting on tea. Would you like a cup?'

'No, thank you.' Mary returned to the relatively safe ground of phone swiping. Jimmy had Googled the opening hours of the local library, she thought, but couldn't be sure, and had possibly bought the latest John Grisham on Amazon. She put the phone down and moved from virtual devices to visible vices. The same ugly ornaments lined the mantle and bookshelves; the carpet still needed a hoover; the windows and curtains were still closed; the box of tissues beside the armchair was almost empty (and he didn't have a cold); the sideboard door was open. Nothing suspicious enough, nothing changed enough. Acute risk score this week: *low*.

Mary relaxed. She'd be out of here in a few minutes. She found herself straightening the wedding picture on the telly and shutting the sideboard door – but something was stuck.

She tried to jam it, and then shuddered when she saw

what looked like skin. Mary opened the door and screamed. There was a baby in the sideboard.

She moved a shaky finger towards the child's arm, which was cold, and weird. And rubber. Mary screamed again, this time with relief. Jimmy's worst case scenario was not happening here today. This was a rubber doll, not a human.

'Jim!'

Cuppa in one hand, the other on his Zimmer frame, Jimmy stopped short in the hall.

'You have an anatomically correct female infant sex doll?' Mary was holding it by the hair. There was no good way to hold it. She put it on the armchair and found herself pulling its antique lace christening dress down over the legs.

'Not a doll; a robot.' Jimmy didn't seem overly concerned that his sex toy had been discovered, or at least he made a good effort not to seem so. He pressed the baby's back and an arm moved up then down again. 'See!' He pressed again, and a little tear dropped from the robot's (not doll's) eye.

It was 9.45 a.m. Mary had a MAPPA at 10.00; no time to do all the things she'd now needed to do as a result of – 'Her name's Emily,' Jimmy said – as a result of Emily. First, she'd have to listen to and note Jimmy's highly logical explanation, and later record it on council and police databases – both of which required passwords and codes and secret keys and fobs and time – a lot of time – that she would not have this afternoon. Her diary, as usual, was angry-full.

Mary took notes as Jimmy explained his right to be with Emily:

- *Thanks to Mary, Jimmy wasn't allowed to have contact with any real children, not even his grandchildren, who he loved, and who loved him.*

- *He wasn't allowed to have a girlfriend either. (That wasn't true. Jimmy just didn't want an adult one.)*
- *He was not even allowed a dog. He loved dogs. He'd never use a puppy to groom children.*
- *Jimmy wasn't allowed to look at the stuff on the internet, and fair enough, after four hundred hours sitting in a circle, he now understood that the children he'd seen were real and maybe not as into the whole thing as they seemed to be.*
- *Emily was legal.*
- *She'd cost him half his savings.*
- *His possession of and affection for the robot – a bit of rubber after all – caused no harm. There were no victims. He had found a legal way thanks to Mary's hard work and the dedication of the groupworkers he'd listened to for four hundred hours, honestly at least a hundred more than was legally required. He had learned to analyse the facts, consider the options, and take the best course of action. For him, finding Emily was like a heroin addict finding methadone. No need to break and enter. A step in the right direction at least, no?*

'It's way worse than creepy, Jimmy. Where did you get it?'

'Online. I had her on order for months. Please don't take her.'

Mary swiped at his phone again. 'You know you're not allowed to delete anything?'

'I didn't. A mate ordered her for me.'

'What mate?'

Jimmy didn't answer.

'Not someone from the group?' It was one of Mary's fears

– that the groupwork her team delivered was most successful in offering the guys a cosy networking environment.

'No.'

'When did you get her … it?'

'Three days ago.'

'And how many times have you used the doll for sex in the last three days?'

'We've spent a lot of time together. I'm so happy, Mary, for the first time since Hilda died.'

Before he'd finished speaking, Mary dialled the Offender Management Unit. 'Hi Minnie, I'm at Jim McKinley's, and I've found a female child robot in his lounge cupboard.' Mary covered the handset because Minnie's response was less than professional. 'Yeah … yep, about five months I guess … Yes, she's called Emily … I know it's not illegal, but there are, like, parts – It's anatomically correct … Yes, that is what I mean. I want you to see this. Can you or someone pop over? I'll get Jim to stay put but I have to go.'

Before getting in her car, Mary checked her work-issue Blackberry. There were three calls from an unknown number, three emails from business support with messages from Macdowall, a missed call from Dr Shearer (who was he?) and one from Fiona Bellwood. There was also a reminder that she had two court reports due at twelve and a MAPPA at ten. It was 9.53 a.m.

The office was buzzing with Wednesday-ness. Wednesday

was the most efficient day of the social worker's week. Most would've tried not to drink Monday and/or Tuesday, and some may have managed. A fair amount of television and sleep was likely to have happened in recent days. Sometimes on Wednesdays an occasional chuckle happened, giving off a whiff of hope that almost masked the regular office smells of off-milk and the sewage place across the way.

Forty or so child-protection workers sat in the pods they were assigned to in the hanger-like space, faces tight and strokes imminent. From what Mary heard as she passed by, Nel was on page twenty of a report recommending that Derek McLaverty should not have any access to his boys if he failed to attend one more session, and/or if any further domestic offending occurred; Daljeep was getting ready to go out on an investigation with Gemma; and Lisa was on the phone, suggesting Carol take her head out of the oven because it was electric and would not have the desired effect.

Please let me get through today without killing a child, they'd all be thinking, as Mary had thought for the last thirty years. *Please help me not ruin a child's life.* She'd prayed each day that she'd get through it without fucking up, without turning out to be the bad guy after all. No-one in the office was expecting fame, riches, or even thanks, even though each worker would have made an excellent protagonist in *It's a Wonderful Life.* They all saved lives, all the time, but no-one ever noticed. Boy did people notice when it went wrong, though. Mary had witnessed at least five of her colleagues do the walk of shame on the same route she was walking now, from one end of this stinky shed to the other, heads low because they had caused a death according to the *Renfield Star* and the *Renfield Star* would know. One, Sharon, had to do the walk of shame for seven weeks before fleeing to Spain, where she relaxed just enough to get cancer. *Look at Sharon*, they all thought as she walked the walk those weeks. *Take a good look, and never, ever, take the mother's word for it.*

There were wonderful moments. Like when eighteen-year-old Vanessa turned up to the office a month ago. Mary had been her social worker from when she was nine months old to when she found a new family at seven. Vanessa had wanted Mary to know that she was now going to college, that she was happy. She showed Mary photos of her boy-friend, a few of her childhood after she was adopted, and one of a box filled with sunglasses.

'These are the ones I gave you?'

When Mary first met Vanessa, she was malnourished and living with her heroin-using mum. Mary had sunglasses on, and the nine-month baby took them off her with glee, chewed at them, and did not want to give them back. Mary let Vanny keep the glasses, which were expensive – Raybans actually – and then wore one three-pound pair each week for the following year.

Those were the moments that made it worthwhile. Looking back, though, Mary was just glad the kid hadn't choked on the wee pins that hold those glasses together. The job was more fun when she knew nothing – like skiing.

Mary reached the other end of the room, where fourteen criminal-justice workers typed court reports and breach reports, updated risk assessments and popped downstairs every hour to check in a service user. 'Service user'! Mary referred to her guys as her guys, and they were all guys. The women were now supervised in a holistic and separatist manner in a different building. Mary found it easier to work with men, but had never been tempted to analyse why. In fact, she wouldn't work with the women, even if you paid her forty K a year.

'Big night last night?' Lil was on her second coffee.

'That obvious?'

'You've put on weight.'

'I know, right? Nine stone fourteen,' said Mary.

'You mean ten stone?' Lil had said a bad word.

'It's the wine. I had three very large glasses at home last night. On my own.'

'Aw, that's so sad.'

'Sad? Are you kidding? Can't believe I've spent all these years getting drunk with other people.'

Lil donned her American movie-trailer voice: 'One alcoholic parole officer. Four weeks to go. One last client. What could possibly go wrong?'

'Mary! MARY!'

Fuck, it was the green-haired student social worker, her voice coming from behind. Mary must not look back. See what happens when she forgot to put on her headphones? She must walk with purpose; she must pretend to be deaf; she must get out the door, across the landing, into the meeting room.

Phew.

Serious folk from serious places sat around a serious desk each month to share the kind of information that should've been shared about Ian Huntley before he murdered two little girls in Soham. Mary could see the girls' innocent faces clearly still; like Vanny's sunglasses, they kept her going. This serious gathering was called the Multi Agency

Public Protection Authority, or MAPPA to people with ADS (Acronym Dependency Syndrome). Mary was able to answer fifty percent of the questions posed about her racist prick lifer guy, Simon Gallacher, who'd murdered an Asian kid when he was an angry white kid, which was just before he turned into an angry white man. Gallacher's criminal record listed a violent offence every five years, most of them racially aggravated. Mary hated his guts and left the meeting with fourteen actions to be completed ASAP. For example:

1. What was the name of Simon Gallacher's Pakistani neighbour, and did the neighbour have a wife or a job or business or relatives or girlfriend or children or car or pets or any contact whatsoever with the *nominal**? (*nominal = evil bastard)
2. Was the Pakistani's* family known***? (*Pakistani = potentially from Pakistan or a place like that) (***known = fucked)
3. Simon Gallacher had commented on Derek McLaverty's Cuck Facebook page. Did they know each other? Had they attended protests or events together?

Mary had thought mostly about noodles throughout the MAPPA. She would get them in Shawlands before making an unscheduled visit to Macdowall, before whatever awfulness she had diarised from 12.30 on.

She stopped at a red light. Time to glance at the diary – there were coded appointments for 12.30 and 1.00 and 1.30 and 2.00 and 2.30 and maybe even 2.45. Her diary was hard to read now with all the changes and additions she'd made,

some in eyeliner. 3.00 and 3.15 and 3.45 and 4.50 and 6.00.
Fucking 6.00? She was supposed to do 'domestic-abuse
modules' with William McInnes from 6.00 until 7.00 at
night, because the fucker worked, had a job, and she wasn't
allowed to discourage that, no matter how inconvenient for
her, nor how little it reduced the likelihood of him fracturing
his wife's skull.

That's right, Mary had set aside an optimistic and for-
ward-thinking thirty minutes to write two court reports
from 12.30 to 1.00, both of which were due at 12.00.

Noodles.

Macdowall didn't answer, so Mary palm-pressed the buzzers
for all eight flats until someone let her in. She managed to
finish most of the noodles before she reached the landing.
Before knocking, Mary peeked through the letterbox (no
obvious sign of life in the hall) and snooped through the
rubbish bag at the door, which was filled with empty beer
and wine bottles. When there was no answer, she checked
under the mat, and then under the small pot plant. The key
was there. She knocked more loudly and was about to give
up when Holly answered the door.

'Is that…?' Mary sniffed at the smoke-filled hall. 'Jesus
Holly, now I'm stoned too. Where's your father? You stayed
here overnight?' Mary barged her way in, and Holly was too
wasted to stop her.

'I didn't stay here. I came this morning to help him
prepare. He has an event at the Edinburgh Book Festival at
two. He's not here. So, can you go? Oi!'

Mary was scanning the living room: two empty wine

bottles, six empty beer cans, at least a dozen joint roaches and a purse, which she peeked inside. The driver's licence belonged to a basic blonde called Fiona Bellwood. Derek McLaverty's HQ was thriving, by the looks. Thousands of posters and flyers added to the t-shirts and books piled on the floor. He'd left his silver MacBook on the dining table. The kitchen had obviously fallen victim to late-night munchies. Mary's prying was determined. She opened the door to the spare bedroom without asking. 'Is Derek staying here?' A photograph of the sons he allegedly loved but never bothered showing up for was on the bedside table. Hanging over a chair was his white t-shirt: *THIS IS WHAT A MRA LOOKS LIKE*. Mary peeked inside the large box on the floor. Inside were the original letters Macdowall wrote to his dead wife.

'Hey, get out,' Holly said.

'Have you seen these?' Underneath the fifty original handwritten letters that had been published was a large A4 envelope with *CUT* written on it. There were around a dozen letters inside the envelope, all of which had been scored through with red pen. 'Some didn't make it into the book, I see. Have you read them?'

Holly grabbed the letters from Mary and followed her as she stormed into the hall. 'You have no respect. How dare you touch other people's things. Do you realise how hard you're making it for my dad? Get out. You are driving him to despair. Do not go in there.'

Too late, Mary had opened the bathroom door, where her son, Jack, was brushing his teeth.

'Hi Mum.'

'Jack? What…?' She stared in disbelief. 'What the *fuck* are you doing here?'

'I could ask you the same.'

'I'm required to visit, by law. How did this happen?'

'Holly and I got friendly.'

'She friended you?'

'We had a drink after the book launch, got chatting on the Cuck page, met up at another event.'

'You stay away from my son.' Mary faced the girl.

'You're invading my personal space,' said Holly.

Mary realised her nose was almost touching Holly's and that she was breaking every rule she'd learned on the four-day conflict resolution course she did in 1983. She called on one of the skills she kind-of-remembered and turned her voice and tone down several notches, which in Mary's opinion made her sound even more aggressive. 'You hear me? You stay away from my son.'

'Mum!' Jack said. 'Leave her alone. Why are you like blaming it all on her.'

Mary turned to Jack. 'Are you really listening to this *Cuck* bullshit? I could tell you a thing or two about that McLaverty; you should beware.'

'Could you, Mary?' Holly said. 'Or would you be breaching confidentiality again?'

Mary ignored her. 'Are you gonna wear one of these t-shirts, Jack?' She was holding the garment with great anger. 'Okay, then, put it on.'

Jack took the t-shirt from her and put it on the basin. 'If you want to know, this bullshit is making me think about things. Like the way you talk to Dad. The way you talk about his work. He is so talented, he's worked so hard for so many years to get where he is, and you call him a colour-in-er-er.'

She was getting hot, but this might not be due to menopause. 'You think I'm abusive?'

Jack took too long to answer. 'All I'm saying is that Liam is worth listening to. That's what I'm doing. Maybe you should try it.'

He'd been brainwashed already. 'Never, ever go near my boy again,' she said to Holly, before making her way to the door.

The traffic lights were against her all the way. Right now, she was stuck behind a black Range Rover, which was also indicating right. Their blinkers were in sync – tick, tick, tick, tick, tick – and Mary found herself tapping to the rhythm on the steering wheel.

Tick, tick, tick, tick, tick.

Tick, tick, tick, tick, tick.

'Hey there Roddie boy.' She tapped a finger per syllable. 'Am I a-bu-sive? Am *I* the arsehole?'

She had called him a colour-in-er-er, after all.

She had made comments about his appearance.

And she had hit him.

The lights changed, and she was relieved when the tick, tick, ticking stopped.

Had hit him! Pffft. A girly lash-out, maybe, a desperate chest-pounding during a desperate time, like when Mary wanted to take over the childcare thing but couldn't because Roddie despised law, and would have hated taking over the money-earning thing. She stopped at the side of the road to get her breath back, but unfortunately could hear what Jack might say, which is exactly what she would say to a client: 'You do realise a girly lash-out is a punch, right? That a chest-pounding is assault?'

Yeah but – size matters, she told herself, and so does fear. Roddie has never been scared.

'Yeah, but.' She sighed – she had heard men say this so many times.

Yeah, but there was no time for this. She had a dangerous criminal to breach.

11

After talking most of it through with Catherine, Mary cleared a few hours. She could do the court reports from home tonight. It was the sheriff and the defence lawyers who wanted them a day before session. The sheriffs never read them anyhow, and the lawyers were dicks. Lil offered to see her other punters, bless her.

For a few hours, Macdowall was the priority. Mary pulled information from Google, Facebook, the Scottish Criminal Records Office (SCRO), the Social Work Information Database (SWID), and the Violent and Sex Offenders Register (shouldn't it be VASOR not VISOR?). She returned calls to Macdowall's GP (ah, that's who Dr Shearer was) and Tracy at the alcohol problem clinic, and Macdowall's 'friend you talked to last night', Fiona Bellwood. None of them was there, so she left messages.

She discovered that Macdowall's probable-shag, Fiona Bellwood, was on the system for destitution (2010), housing issues (2012) and drug counselling (2012/2014, cannabis/amphetamines). Mary emailed a referral to the child-protection first-response team, outlining the potential risk and recommending a visit to Fiona Bellwood and an assessment of the situation.

Mary decided to omit one tiny detail in the breach report, a little personal development no-one needed to know about – that Jack was now involved with the Macdowalls and the Cuck movement. It was her fault. She should have stopped him going into the book launch. No need to mention Jack; definitely no need. She concluded the breach as follows:

Mr Macdowall failed to attend his first appointment with me, orchestrating and prioritising a men's rights rally at the prison instead. Three people were arrested at this rally, according to BBC News. Mr Macdowall openly consumed alcohol at his book launch the night of his release, and as far as I know he has been drinking heavily since (see photos attached to the Cuck Facebook Page, link below, and the photograph I have attached of the cup he drank from on the evening of his book launch). He failed to attend his second office appointment with me yesterday at 9.00 a.m. Later that night, he found a way to contact me on my private Facebook page. He appeared to be under the influence of alcohol and perhaps other substances and asked me if he could have sex with a Ms Fiona Bellwood, a single mother who he had only just met earlier that day. Ms Bellwood is known to social work for drug misuse issues and reported to me that she has a son, now twelve. I have reason to believe Mr Macdowall ignored my directions and spent the evening with Ms Bellwood anyway.

When I visited Mr Macdowall's house this morning, there was evidence of Ms Bellwood (she had left her purse in the living room), and of heavy drinking (empty wine and beer bottles) and drug use (distinct smell of cannabis and drug-using paraphernalia).

Mr Macdowall is appearing at a heavily publicised sold-out event at the Edinburgh Book Festival at 2.00 p.m. today, and news feeds are already reporting that angry protestors are gathering at Charlotte Square. Since his third month in custody, Macdowall has become heavily involved with men's rights movement, in particular with its Scottish leader, Derek McLaverty, who is the publisher of Macdowall's "book", Cuck – Letters to

My Dead Wife, *a publication that highlights the nominal's narcissism, misogyny and lack of remorse for his actions. McLaverty has seven previous violent convictions for assault/serious assault/ assault to permanent disfigurement and endangerment of life, all of which were aggravated by hate crime (domestic, racial, homophobic). Mr McLaverty's interests appear to extend beyond those related to fair custody rights, to an ideology which supports racial hatred.*

I am extremely concerned by Mr Macdowall's audacious and hostile attitude. He is not attending supervision, he is drinking heavily, and may be having casual relations with an unknown and potentially vulnerable single mother. In my opinion, Mr Macdowall may also be involved in the wider and more sinister interests of the alt-right movement, or he is being used and swept along by its conductors. Either way, I feel that serious harm is imminent and in order to protect the public, I recommend Mr Macdowall be recalled to prison immediately.

Happy with her facts and her writing and her assessment, Mary attached the 'Macdowall.17' breach report to the secure email addresses of the parole board, MAPPA, and her boss, Catherine. She marked it 'urgent', and almost pressed 'send', pausing to reflect that she shouldn't send it yet. She should read it again, one more time. She should breathe.

Mary longed to stop reflecting. To do a thing and not reflect on it.

Mary reflected that she needed to be one step above 'defensible' in court, and so before pressing 'send' she dialled Macdowall's mobile number, the one she had asked him for and had written down and managed to put in her work-issue Blackberry. That's right, she good old-fashioned dialled it, having decided it was probable her report was fair. On balance. Considering.

She was confident! About the essence. So much so that she would read the report to Macdowall right now, right here, over the phone, totally out loud. That's what she'd do: read the breach to her nominal.

'Liam, is that you?'

He sounded happy, like he'd had a drink, and this made Mary relax. She was doing the right thing.

Macdowall said something about a 'lurt' and free wine and nosh. Mary could hear the clinking of cutlery. 'I'm so sorry, can I call back?'

'No. Stop whatever it is you're doing. Go somewhere quiet.'

'What? (Yum, thank you! Yes please.)'

Mary could hear a drink being poured. He was obviously being served, superstar. 'I'll take this out to the smoking area, hang on. Okay I'm – I'll go to the author toilets.'

The *author* toilets. Fancy.

'Okay, sorry, Mary. I'm sitting on a Portaloo. What is it?'

'Liam, you've done almost everything wrong since you got out, you do realise that? It can hardly be a shock. You're breached.'

A moment's pause. 'I'm what?'

'I'm going to read you the conclusion of the report I'm sending to the parole board after this call. Okay?' Mary found herself revising and deleting as she went along. If she couldn't say it out loud to Macdowall, she should get rid of it. And she did; bits anyway. 'This is the conclusion: "I am concerned that Mr Macdowall is not complying with the conditions of his licence. I can confirm that he has not attended two scheduled supervision appointments, I have photographic and physical evidence that he is drinking, and believe he may be having casual relations with a single mother who is known to the social work department.'"

'Oh God, oh God.' Macdowall kept saying. 'Oh God'. A lock slid, which gave Mary time to edit the next bit.

"'I am also concerned that he may be attracted to, or drawn into, potentially violent situations because of his sudden fame and association with known anti-immigration and anti-feminist activists. To protect the public, I recommend Mr Macdowall be recalled to prison immediately.'"

Mary heard the clinking of cutlery. 'Liam, I'm heading to Charlotte Square now. I'll meet you at the signing table around 3.00 p.m., after the event, okay?'

All he said was, 'Oh God,' then the phone went dead.

12

As Mary passed the exit for Lowfield, she was minded of her very first prison visit with Maggie, her practice teacher, thirty years earlier. Maggie had a court-report interview at 11.00, and yet she seemed relaxed when the probation review still wasn't finished at 10.25, even though it would take at least forty minutes to get from the office to the prison by car. Maggie even got petrol on the way, plus a sandwich, which she ate while driving at high speed on the motorway with no sat nav, while also chatting to Mary, while listening to Clyde 1, occasionally singing along and navigating by eye to the prison, which was in the middle of nowhere.

Mary had not managed to do more than three things at once for at least a year, and when she did manage, it was with a great deal of stress and unhappiness, mostly for those in her vicinity. However, she still managed two things sometimes, like making a hands-free call while driving. She tried that now. 'Jack?'

'Hi, Mum.' The words were even less enthusiastic than they'd been in Macdowall's bathroom earlier. *Macdowall's* bathroom, Jesus. She was so tempted to scream at her little boy, who used to chuckle so hard when she tickled him.

'Where are you?'

'Train.'

'Where to?'

'Edinburgh, with Holly.'

Holly? Edinburgh. Jesus Christ. 'I'm heading to Liam's

event too. Can we talk later? Meet in the foyer after three? Are you okay?'

'Sure, bye.' He hung up.

The temperature in the car suddenly increased by about fifteen degrees. Mary put the air-conditioning on high and opened all the windows. When she was in her twenties, Mary didn't think childbirth'd be a big deal, not till she shat ten pounds out of her fanny at twenty-eight. Her pain threshold, much to her surprise, turned out to be low. Until one year ago, Mary didn't believe the tales old women told about the menopause. What was the problem with getting hot? Mary often got hot, sometimes very. Turns out a hot flush was like an orgasm. If you're not sure you've had one, you haven't.

She decided to call her boss, Catherine. 'Hi, it's Mary. Can you ring me? I'm not quite coping.'

She felt better having left the message, better enough to listen to umpteen voicemails from, then return calls to:

Roddie:

'Roddie?'

Roddie:

'Where are you?'

Dr Shearer's Terrifying Receptionist:

'Hi, this is Mary Shields from Renfield Social Work. Can I please speak with Dr Shearer? It's about Liam Macdowall, whose life licence I supervise … I'm driving, so I can't fax you a consent form now. Criminal Justice Social Work, Renfield. Yes, he has. But I can't. I'm on the M8. Mary Shields. Social Worker, Yes, but … But Dr Shearer called me. He actually wants to speak to me – much more than I do to him. Okay, fine, can you please get him to call me, then? He can call me at 2.07? Until what time, 2.09? Fine, 2.07. Okay thanks. I'll be at an event, so I might need to call him back. What if it takes me more than two minutes to call back? Okay, I'll keep my phone on.'

Detective Sergeant Minnie Johnstone:

'What do you mean there was no doll at McKinley's? It was on the armchair, in an embroidered dress. Her name's Emily. Well, can you check again? Look in the bins. Can you get a warrant?'

The Bored Sheriff's Clerk and four other court-report-related people:

'I'll get the reports in for court tomorrow morning. Sorry, work emergency.'

Roddie (by text):

You're being a cunt. Is it over? I'm driving on a motorway at high speed and it feels like it's fucking over.

Roddie:

'Where are you?' (*Crying*) 'Please call me.'

Mary took the next exit and screeched to a halt in the services carpark. Her hands were shaking, there were sweat marks under her arms and (even worse) under her meno-pausally enhanced boobs. The car seemed to be shrinking, its sides pushing in, smaller and smaller, yet she was getting heavier. Soon she would *be* the car, soon there'd be no point trying to breathe. That'd be a relief.

Mary had only learned to recognise a panic attack in recent months but had probably been having minor ones since she was a child. She breathed in for five, then rang her boss, Catherine, who answered this time: 'Hi Cath, I'm not well. I need some time off.'

'But you'll be leaving—'

'I'm not coping. I need a rest, just for a couple of days.'

'What's wrong? Is there anything I can do?'

For thirty years, Mary had encouraged her clients to be articulate and confident about their ailments when attending an intimidating and oft-times embarrassing eight-minute GP appointment. Mary was shocked when she herself had failed spectacularly on her last visit to the doctor. She had been practising since: 'For the last eighteen months, I've had increasingly profound anxiety, rapid mood swings, poor concentration, a growing alcohol dependency, nausea, diarrhoea, constant fatigue, poor sleep patterns, night sweats, regular and increasingly scary panic attacks – including one on the motorway just now – heart palpitations, hot flushes, a dry fanny and sore tits. In a nutshell, I am suffering from The Menopause. And yes, you could help by telling me to go home to bed immediately.'

'Have you eaten?' There was a distinct lack of understanding in Catherine's tone.

'You'll get the menopause too one day, you know,' said Mary.

'Ach, they'll have cured it by then.'

'I need to go home, I really do.'

'You know what this means, though, don't you?'

'It means I'm fucking sick.'

'Stage four, Mary. No-one in our team has ever reached stage four. If you leave on sick, you'll never get back in.'

'Shove your stages up your arse. I'm going home.'

Catherine sighed. She would now have to implement

stage-four procedures, which were probably pretty complicated, as well as write two letters to court, and do-or-delegate
the thirty-six other things Mary had unrealistically scheduled for the rest of the week. 'Right, okay. So can you go
to the festival first, if you're up to it? Are you? Make sure
nothing bad happens? It's too late for me to get anyone else
to go. Big Bob's even calling me about this; it's big news. Two
officers will meet you at the entrance to the event. What's
your ETA?'

'Sat nav says thirty minutes.'

'I'll let them know. They're going to arrest him at three,
on the way out. Ring me straight after and we'll go through
your diary. You'll need a medical certificate if you're off till
Friday. I want to see you Monday. Do you think your GP
can confirm what's wrong? That you have *The Menopause?*'

Mary paused – 'Yes. I reckon he fucking well can' – and
screeched out of the carpark as fast as she'd screeched in. The
difference between how she felt before she arrived was huge
as well as miniscule. She had the same amount of adrenaline
right now, but she was using it like she did when she was
young, excited, infatuated, a new homeowner, a new mum;
she was channelling it into driving too fast; into hating her
boss, Catherine, who had not suggested kindly that she
should about-face and go to bed; into hating McKinley
and his disappearing baby-sex-bot; into hating Dr Shearer's
Terrifying Receptionist, who could easily have put the god-
doctor-figure on the phone but didn't because she had the
power not to; and into hating Dr Liam Macdowall and his
prick of a daughter, both of whom had somehow managed
to weasel their way into her beautiful boy's life. *Just you dare,
you screwed up cunts, just you dare.*

13

Mary battled through the festival traffic to Princes Street but couldn't turn left into Charlotte Square. She could see from her car that the festival and surrounds had been overtaken by chanting protestors, who were, at this stage, peaceful, the two teams walking round the square in opposite directions, thus far without collision. Men's rights activists and co. walked clockwise; feminists et cetera walked anticlockwise. Mary wondered if they'd tossed for it. Police dotted either side of the road. The two teams were almost equal in their chants.

She headed down to Roddie's old haunt, Stockbridge, to find a park. It was 2.00 p.m. The gig would have started already. Mary decided to sprint up the hill to town, well a Munro rather than a hill, as it turned out, disguised by excellent architecture. Mary used to be able to run for miles. She sometimes wondered if running could still be her thing, if she trained. Maybe running would be the thing she'd be *known* for.

Her work-issue Blackberry buzzed halfway up Mont de Stockbridge. Mary decided to answer as an excuse to rest.

'Hi Mary, it's Doctor Shearer. I've been trying to reach you since Friday. Liam Macdowall didn't collect his prescription for sertraline after his release, as planned. He got them this morning. The pharmacist said he looked a little under the influence of alcohol.'

'So, he hasn't had his meds since he got out?'

'That's what I'm saying.'

'And this morning he got a whole packet?'

'That's what I'm—'

She sprinted up the hill and pushed past the police who lined the square. She bashed through the ever-thicker counter-flowing placards, some of which were bumping into each other now, and ran into the foyer. Macdowall's event was advertised on the screens in the corners: SOLD OUT.

Mary flashed her ID and said with great importance: 'Let me through. Let me through. My name's Mary Shields. I'm Liam Macdowall's supervising officer.'

'Who?' The teenage gatekeeper body-blocked her. She almost fell over.

'I supervise Liam Macdowall's life licence.'

He looked at her as if she was speaking Russian. 'Have you got a ticket?'

Mary barged through into the body of the festival and ran round the boardwalk till she found the venue. The huge marquee was packed. People were standing at the back, and several journalists, as well as Derek McLaverty, buzzed round the entrance. The audience members were chatting and fidgeting, and the stage was empty.

'Where is he?' she asked Derek.

'Well if it isn't Mary,' Derek said.

'Where's Liam?'

'He's coming. He's in the loo. Why? Something wrong? Why are you here?'

'Where are the authors' toilets?' Mary asked.

Derek and a few others followed her as she ran to the tent across the boardwalk.

Inside the yurt, food and wine and cutlery were laid out. This must have been where Macdowall was being served when she rang earlier. Outside there was a pretty smokers' area for writers and festival officials. In the corner sat a small Portakabin labelled: *Authors' Toilets*. Mary ran into the men's.

Two festival officials were already in there. Derek followed Mary inside.

'He said he had a sore stomach, so we left him to it,' said one. 'I think he might have fainted.'

The end door was closed.

'Liam? Liam, are you in there?' She bent down to look under the door, but there was no space, only something dark.

'LIAM!' Mary banged at the door, then kicked it, but it was no use.

Derek pushed Mary aside to kick with his male foot, which he hurt in the process. The door did not budge.

'Get someone strong!' she ordered. 'Call 999.'

She kicked the door once more, but kickboxing wasn't going to be the thing that Mary would be remembered for. As she kicked a third time, she already knew how she'd be remembered. Not by little Vanny and the sunglasses, or singing, or stand-up comedy or running, but by a toilet cubicle.

A thick pool of blood oozed out when the door opened. On the floor was Macdowall's satchel, an empty bottle of red, a phone, and an empty packet of antidepressants. On the toilet was Macdowall, his wrists gouged with a dinner knife, his eyes open. On the wall behind him, in thick blood, Macdowall had scrawled an enormous letter C.

PART TWO

THE NED

14

Half of Mary's lunch hit a man called Ian, and the crowd in the courtyard clamoured to help. 'Ian, oh my God!' 'I've got a hanky!' 'Here's a tissue!' Mary was concentrating on keeping the rest of the noodles down and couldn't think of a famous Ian.

'Quick, come with me.' A suave twenty-something took Mary's hand and pushed his way from the step outside the authors' toilets into the red velvet of the inner yurt, depositing her on a luxurious bench and shoving a hessian bag in her face. Mary decided to put her head inside it, which sated twenty-something guy. 'In for four, hold for seven, out for eight. That's it. What a thing to see. Poor you.'

'Are you Mary Shields?' A policewoman had entered the inner yurt, which was basically an enormous vagina: soft, red velvet benches, draped ceilings, pulsating pellet stove in the corner.

Mary took her head out of the bag. 'I am. I'm Mary Shields.' Her name sounded heavy and was downright sinister written down. Even Mary's address seemed to have an edge – 20 Mansion House Square; it scanned with 25 Cromwell Street. The police officer also wrote down her date of birth, her telephone numbers, her employer info, contact details for Roddie, and a brief statement.

The officer pointed to a woman sitting nearby. 'You and Margaret need to stay here for now,' she said. 'We'll get you out soon. It's just neds, nothing to be alarmed about. You should know they've removed the body but the area has all been sealed off. Can I've a minute Bob?'

'Sure thing,' said twenty-something Bob, who reclaimed his hessian bag and stood. 'Ladies, while you wait there's whisky, tablet and oysters plucked from under the kilts of clansmen. Mary, doll, you get to hang with Margaret. How cool is that?'

Margaret, sitting opposite, was obviously famous like Ian. She was around seventy, wore long boots, leggings and an oversized shirt, and sported a spectacular fuzz-ball of silver hair.

'I can look after myself,' she said when Bob had gone. 'But are you okay?' Her accent was American, or Canadian.

You should always say Canadian first, Mary thought to herself, in case she accidentally asked the question out loud. Canadian first. 'Fine thanks.' Mary had managed to not say it. She scanned her busy head for famous Margarets and only one came to mind: English, and dead, thankfully. Mary's cheeks were wet. She reached into her bag for a tissue and noticed her work-issue Blackberry was buzzing. Her hand shook as she lifted it, but the messages were all from before 2.00 p.m. – a comforting time to be from. One was from Detective Sergeant Minnie Mouse, who'd been unable to locate McKinley's child sex robot and wanted to do an unannounced joint visit tomorrow if poss – how about 9.00 a.m.? There were messages regarding overdue MAPPA paperwork and incomplete LS/CMI risk assessments and late CPO review reports and absence of up-to-date SWID case notes and new mileage forms and a reminder to put all interviews and visits on VISOR. There were several messages from clients about appointments, and an email from her boss, Catherine:

Mary, I am so sorry, but I can't get anyone to do the report for John Paul O'Donnell tomorrow. I'd do it, but I've got a MAPPA2. If it's not done, he'll stay in custody another three weeks. He's ex-Looked After. Can you nip to Lowfield at 10 and write it at home? I've booked you in. CJSW done 12m ago, attached, also SCRO, SWID and CPCC. Maybe defer for DTTO? Or CPO w RDS, poss RAMH to beef it up?

Mary understood every letter, and they comforted her. She could do that, sure. There was no disaster here. No blast radius rippling out already. Tomorrow would just be another Thursday. She'd go to prison for the interview with John Paul and make a surprise joint visit to McKinley on the way. She messaged Catherine and Minnie to let them know, then opened the attachments her boss had sent, calming herself with the personal history of twenty-one-year-old John Paul O'Donnell, a coke-addled ned whose life was way worse than hers, even now, and who she'd be meeting for the first time tomorrow.

She was breathing steadily again when Margaret nudged her with a whisky tumbler. 'I suggest you drink.'

Mary became aware of the noise around her. Fire sirens had joined the angry orchestra in Charlotte Square. She took the whisky from famous Margaret.

'I think we're going to be here a while.' Margaret sat beside her and took a sip of her own whisky. 'Don't know how safe we're s'posed to feel with just canvas between us and them.'

'I love your work,' Mary used her limited powers of speech to say. She prayed that Margaret Whoever didn't ask which work in particular, because she hadn't read anything made-up since the world forced her to devour *The Da Vinci Code* in 2003.

'Thank you.' The lady author poured another drink in a manner befitting a very important Margaret.

The chanting was getting louder. Male voices, moving closer; they couldn't be more than metres away. Mary could hear the words now – 'Feminazi!' 'Misandrist Mary!' 'Man-Killer Mary!'

'What? Who are they talking about?'

'I'm afraid you are the Mary to whom the gentlemen refer,' said wise Margaret, whose surname was on the tip of Mary's tongue.

'But they don't know me.'

She handed Mary her iPad, which was open on the Cuck Facebook page. 'He posted this just before he did the world a great service, and tagged you. Drink this.' Margaret handed her another whisky, which Mary gulped before reading:

'THE LAST LETTER

I thought I'd worked it all out, ha, found my tribe. You're right about me.

I am an idiot,

Unfortunately.

Liam xx'

In her head, Mary was explaining her actions to a jury. Macdowall had tagged her as an ironic nod to one of his understandably stringent life-licence conditions, she would argue (i.e., that he must inform his supervising officer of any change of address, which was now nowhere). That was all, nothing more significant than that. The next question was more difficult to defend: *Then explain to the court, Mrs Shields, why Macdowall's last words mirror those he inscribed in your hardback copy of his book on the evening of his launch? I.e., 'To Mary, who's not an idiot, Unfortunately.'*

Mary would have to burn the book.

What was she thinking?

She'd have to burn the book.

Mary grabbed her personal mobile from her bag, which, as usual for a work day, was on silent. The screen was spurting alerts, but she phoned Jack before looking at them. He didn't answer, so she left a message and a text: *Pls get in touch. Need to know ur ok. I'm in the yurt. xx*

Mary had been advised to change her Facebook name to something obscure or to at least set her privacy to 'friends only', but she hadn't bothered. Her offenders were rarely held back by settings, she'd found. She had 343 Facebook message requests, twenty-three direct messages from friends, or friends of friends, and more friend requests than the 154 she already had. An awful picture kept popping up on her timeline, of a middle-aged woman with bile on her chin and boob sweat. It took Mary a few glances to recognise herself. The photo and accompanying article were posted ten minutes ago by Derek McLaverty on his blog, The Lion's Roar. It had been shared 123 times, 124...

'That's me.'

''Fraid so,' said Margaret.

'I've got batwings.' Mary had zoomed in on an arm. 'I've spent the last thirty years preventing other people's worst case scenarios and this is mine.'

'Fat arms?'

For quite a while, Mary thought she might have something to say, and Margaret was patient. It was a relief when a team arrived to take the woman home. Before heading off, she leaned down and whispered in Mary's ear: 'A lot of people kill themselves. Some of them are good, others are arseholes.'

'I can escort you out now,' the police officer said to Mary. 'Where's your car?'

'It's, um over in Stockbridge, but—' She had to walk and talk: past the courtyard, which was flickering with fluorescent jackets, and across the boardwalk to a small gate on the now-quiet side of the square.

'You okay if I leave you here?' The officer said, having kindly walked her at least a block away from the festival.

'Yeah, but the thing is, I had whisky, in the tent, cos of nerves. Do you have a breathalyser?'

The police officer did not, and suggested Mary get the train.

Mary tested herself as she walked to Stockbridge. Post hurl she had downed three whiskies with her probably legendary BFF. To assess the gravity of the situation, she leaned on Dean Bridge, closed her eyes, and counted from one. Inebriation score: ten. That was, her head was spinning by the time she got to ten.

There was only one way out of this: sambuca. Mary had never managed the fingers-down-the-throat thing. She'd tried very hard, Roddie or Lil often encouraging from behind: 'Don't bring 'em out yet, work through, hold, hold!' She couldn't do it, unless she had a sambuca first. It gave her that extra gag factor. She phoned Jack as she walked. No answer, so she texted:

Pls let me know you're okay. I'm heading back to Glasgow soon if you want a lift.

He texted back straight away: *Wtf have you done?*

Had someone ignited her face? Mary fanned herself:
What do you mean?

She grabbed the Cuck PR itinerary from her bag. Derek McLaverty's mobile number was listed on the front page, and she rang it immediately.

'Derek, it's Mary Shields. Please don't hang up. I'm ringing to see if you're okay.'

'Mary Shields.' He must have been on the train. Mary could hear the Glasgow Central announcement and lots of loud talking. Was that Jack in the background?

'I'm fine, thank you,' he said.

'I wanted to say how sorry I am about Liam. I know how much you meant to each other.'

This wasn't true. She just wanted to diffuse the situation, get him on side, and she wanted to find Jack. Was that his voice? She could hear him. 'Is Jack there with you, by any chance?' she asked. 'Can you put him on?'

Derek muffled the handset. A moment later: 'He doesn't want to talk, Mary.'

'Put him on,' she said.

'He doesn't want to talk to you. That's awful isn't it? Losing contact with your child.'

'It's been a hard day, Derek; a very sad day,' she said.

'Indeed, and hugging your baby would help, no doubt. I understand. In fact, I feel the same. I need to hug my boys.'

'Are you going there now?'

'Thanks for your concern, Mary.' He hung up.

Walking into the first bar she found, Mary rang the police and Nel to inform them that McLaverty was about to breach the bail condition prohibiting him from going near his ex-wife's address.

'Sambuca,' Mary said to the bartender. She gulped it down, grimaced, and raced to the toilet.

15

Mary drove home with all the windows open and with tears streaming, freaking out every time she saw a police car or heard a siren. The first thing she did when she got in was light a pre-rolled joint, which she held with a violently shaking hand and sucked the life out of. The landline was ringing. The landline never rang. Mary moved towards it as if she were a young blonde in the first scene of a horror movie.

It was Roddie. He'd been worried about her for days, had finally managed to cancel his last events and was on his way home. 'I know what's happened. I've spoken to Jack. He's fine. Turn all your devices off. Don't read any of it. It's nonsense and you're going to be okay. You've done nothing wrong.'

Roddie existed: thank God. It took her a while to make a word. 'Promise?'

'I promise. Tagging you was his manipulative grande finale. Prize arsehole. I'll be home tomorrow afternoon. Go to the doctor first thing, please. Stay in and rest till I'm there.'

'I've got a report and a visit.'

'You're leaving! You don't need this bullshit anymore. Boarding, gotta go. Don't go online. I love you Mary Shields.'

And with that, her name sounded light again.

Mary woke to Samantha's operatic orgasm. *Sex and the City* had been on repeat all night.

8.30 a.m. Shit. As usual for the last eighteen months, her pants and vest were dripping wet, a creek flowing through her new cleavage and pooling on her new tummy. She scraped her drenched clothes and sheets off and put them in the wash, peed, showered, tossed on jeans and a t-shirt, and headed to the kitchen to begin gathering the day's essentials. A three-quarter empty bottle of Sangiovese, sitting on the floor next to the bin, triggered a memory from a hitherto forgotten last night. Mary had decided to throw the wine in the bin, but must have been side-tracked, perhaps with the jigsaw puzzle. That was right. She'd turned all her devices off, as Roddie had advised, and become a little intoxicated. A pair of scissors, now spread-eagled on the table, had been used by Mary to amputate several family homes in Vernazza, which she had then forced into un-natural bonds with villagers in Monterosso. A large pile of ashes, and some fragments of the hardcover copy of *Cuck*, lay in the hearth. She'd had a book-burning ceremony too, which had turned out to be quite hypnotic. Mary grabbed her phone, charger, bag, ID, and work-issue Blackberry, chucked them in her work satchel, and headed to McKinley's.

Minnie hadn't shown yet. It was ten past nine, and the wait had weakened Mary's resolve to avoid the internet. Her personal mobile was charging, and she was reading the texts on her work-issue Blackberry. Catherine, her boss, wanted her to call urgently, so she tried, failed, left a message. Minnie texted: *In light of yesterday, let's reschedule. Hope you're okay.*

Bugger. She'd come all this way. Wasted an hour already. Could've written a full CJSWR, at least done the LS/CMI or whisked off a few CPORs. If she'd known. What a waste of time. Mary didn't waste time, which is why she was knocking on McKinley's door.

As usual, he was holding on to his Zimmer. No ball/s this time, but a wet spot on his boxers, which Mary must not think about for many, many years to come.

'Put some trousers on.' Mary had never used this tone with McKinley before. She followed his saggy bottom as he shuffled through the hall.

'Where are your trousers kept?' She'd entered his bedroom without permission, which was stupid of her, especially considering he and the Zimmer were now at the door, blocking her exit.

'Top drawer.'

Mary grabbed a neatly ironed pair of pyjama bottoms. Nothing dodgy in the drawer, as far as she could see. She walked towards the door, assuming Jimmy would move out of the way. He didn't.

'Get out of the way, Jimmy.' Mary put her hands on the front bar of his walker and pushed. He pushed back for a while, like a dad pretending to arm-wrestle his child, then, thankfully, shuffled back and out of the way.

Safely in the hall, Mary said: 'So where did you put it?'

'What?'

'The child sex doll.' She'd said doll not robot deliberately, to enrage and entrap him.

'I have no idea what you're talking about,' Jimmy said.

'Where is Emily?'

'Who?'

They stared each other out as she moved towards him. 'Really?' She wouldn't have blinked first if she'd had time to wash off yesterday's mascara. 'Go and put these on, Jimmy.'

Mary pried one of his hands from the walker and placed the pyjama bottoms in it. 'We'll wait for you in the living room.' By 'we', Mary meant her and the Zimmer, which she yanked from McKinley out of badness. Let the fucker fall over.

Mary parked the Zimmer beside McKinley's armchair, and the wheels slid into a pair of grooves in the carpet. This was its place. The armchair, with extending leg and retractable back, was McKinley's place. Mary scanned the room for signs of deviance, like Emily, and got madder each second. To look her in the eye and say: 'I have no idea what you're talking about.' She was too emotional, too angry. She shouldn't be here alone; she should leave. She steadied herself by holding the rubber handles of Jimmy's walker, one of which was coming loose. Mary found herself pulling at the loose handle, which came off easily. She looked inside the hollow metal tube. There was something there, but her fingers were too fat to get a grasp. She lifted the Zimmer and wriggled.

A pen drive.

She should ring the police and wait for them to arrive before confronting Jimmy. But she had to be at Lowfield for 10.00 or some kid would stay in jail another three weeks. She should ring the police and let them know, but that's what she did when she found Emily. Look how that had turned out. Mary put the pen drive in her jeans pocket, replaced the rubber handle, and raced to the door.

'I have to go, Jimmy.' She was in her car in four seconds max.

Just Thursday, Mary said to herself as she started her car.

Thursdays were always awful. Monday Social Worker always believed too strongly in the ability and energy of Thursday Social Worker, and it always ended in severe discontent. *Just Thursday. Just Thursday. Just Thursday*, Mary chanted, engine on, sweat dripping from her chin and ears. Her mobile beeped, and if she hadn't looked at it, maybe that's what today would've been: Just Thursday.

She drove home immediately and worked quickly: sweeping ashes and bits of pages into plastic bags, flushing three full buds of green down the loo, taking bags of bottle-clanging rubbish to the bins. She'd read enough on her phone in the car to expect a knock on the door soon. She was all over the internet. 'Manhater should be done for manslaughter', Derek McLaverty and his lions were arguing, and people were hearing them roar.

'Misandrist Mary called me last night', Derek had somehow posted from his cell, 'all weepy, weepy, trying to get me on side. But I know her game, that emotional manipulation. Typical woman, asking questions all nicey-nicey but really it's a trap. When she hung up, she shopped me for needing a hug from my boys, and now I'm locked up again. Because my best friend was *murdered* and I needed to hug my sons.

'Funny fact: Mary-Contrary's son, Jack Shields-Lawson, hates her guts! We welcome you, Jack, to our movement. Things have to change, folks. Liam's dead because he wanted a life, and I'm inside because I love my children.'

She shouldn't have clicked on the video of Derek being interviewed on YouTube, winning every argument with the presenter, who passed articulate and collected £200 in round one, and subsequently said all the wrong things, just as Mary was now thinking all the wrong things, like Derek

McLaverty was the scum of the earth. That cool demeanour, that designer suit, that bullshit USP – being a devoted dad of two when he couldn't even set aside an hour a week to see them.

Whatever. Later. She had to be at Lowfield in fifteen minutes. Drugs defo gone, windows open, sex toys in drawer, laptop search history deleted, she reached for her key, and remembered the pen drive in her pocket. Shit, the pen drive. She should deal with that as a matter of urgency. She couldn't take it to prison. Mary raced back into her bedroom, opened the rarely used drawer under her bed filled with heeled boots she wanted to wear but never did because they didn't suit her, and placed the pen drive in one of her favourites. From River Island, they were – kind of retro, maybe if she tried them with a maxi skirt.

On the way to prison, she left a message asking Minnie to call her, and another with her boss, Catherine. She arrived at Lowfield at three minutes past ten.

A drop of head sweat fell on the officer's shoe while Mary was being scanned, but she was kind enough to ignore it, and escorted her through to the agent's area. John Paul hadn't been processed yet, so she had time to look at the court report, compiled two months ago by Sylvia, sixty-three, who refused to type her own reports, dictating into a tape recorder for a typist to finish off. She was regularly called to meetings for referring to the business-support workers as typists. Sylvia's oration was far from flowing – the business-support workers' goodwill and hearing seriously deficient – making the end product rarely meaningful. John Paul was in court two months ago for police assault, and Sylvia's account of the offence read thus:

'Mr O'Donnell informed the writer that on the night of the offence he had consumed three pints of lager and spent approximately eighty pounds on cocaine, which he had earned selling furniture on Gumtree, which he also consumed. When he presented at the police station around 2.00 a.m. he was by admission probably intoxicated. He informed the writer he recalls losing his phone sometime around getting a chippy at approximately 9.00 p.m. and the next thing finding himself with his shirt off at Govan police station yelling his phone number, over and over, 0734382459, 0734382459, et cetera. While Mr O'Donnell did not deny that he probably committed the offence in the interview with the writer, which is why he pled guilty, he found it difficult to express remorse because he (his words) 'cannae mind for f*'s sake close inverted commas.'

No wonder Sheriff Mackay hated social workers! Mary scanned the background section for anything that made sense.

'John Paul's mother died of a heroin overdose when he was a baby.'

'Lived with his Grandpa Joseph, a road worker, and was very happy till he carked it.'

'Got into music with his grandpa, still into it.'

His grandpa was Joseph O'Donnell! In Mary's mind, John Paul's grandpa was an elderly man behind a tobacco counter, but he was Mary's age, or would be if he hadn't been run over by a truck when John Paul was fourteen. Fourteen: bad age, for a boy. If shit goes down at home and you happen to be fourteen, you're fucked.

Mary had been a big part of Joseph's life for a year after he took over the care of JP, as they called the baby then. During one of Mary's manic clear-outs, she gave Joseph her vinyl collection as a prize for doing everything right and therefore being free of social work forever. Joseph put on Dire Straits, held baby JP and danced round the living room singing with joy. Mary remembered the baby's bright eyes and his meaty chuckle. He was inclined to be happy, that kid.

The baby, now twenty-one, was approaching. His eyes were still bright, but for different reasons. He did not look inclined to be happy. He sat with a grunt, spread his legs as wide apart as possible and crossed his arms.

'Hi there, I'm Mary Shields.' She extended her hand to shake John Paul's, having decided many years ago that she'd rather risk getting hep C than be an arsehole.

Eventually, John Paul unlocked his arms and offered his hand, which was shaky, and dripping with sweat. 'How long will this take?'

Men often entered these rooms angry, filled with distressing problems that it was too late to get help with, fully expecting another telling-off, another putting-down. Last week, she interviewed accidental murderer William Smith, for example. When he walked in, he looked like he could have murdered again, on purpose this time. William had crossed his arms and remained silent for five minutes. At the fifteen-minute mark he was crying because Mary had asked and listened and was coming up with some ideas. Angry didn't scare Mary. You could do something with angry.

'It'll take three, three and a half hours. Why, do you have a date? In D Hall?'

'Ha ha.'

Perhaps he was inclined towards happiness after all.

'Just I have an AA meeting at eleven.' He looked like every twenty-one-year-old she'd met in this place: a raw, angry, terrified kid trying his best to get on with his first stint in an adult jail, fully expecting it would not be his last.

'You can refuse the interview if you like. I'm not forcing you.' *Please refuse!* Then she wouldn't have to do it. Why wasn't she home in bed?

'No, no, just that. It's good, the AA and all that. Don't want to miss it.'

Mary laid out her papers on the table and clicked her pen. 'I'll be as fast as I can. Mostly we need to talk about the offence and sentencing options. I have a recent report here, so I don't need to go through your whole history. Just tell me about the fishfingers and we'll take it from there.' She wrote his name in capitals at the top of her pad: 'No hyphen, two n's, two l's?'

John Paul was looking at the prison officer in the corridor. 'Can I check with Dawn about going straight to AA?'

Cocaine or thereabouts had shrivelled his pupils, and Mary wondered if the wriggling meant prison piles, which might be a thing.

'You can check with Dawn in a few minutes, okay? John Paul? Can you please look me in the eyes, just for a moment … at me. Ooo, way too long. Left, up, right, back a bit, good. You're off your face, and I don't blame you. I'd do the same. But if we don't get this report done you'll get a custodial tomorrow. Or do you prefer prison?' Mary asked this question all the time and, sadly, more than fifty percent of respondents, including John Paul, said something like: 'I'd never admit to that.'

Most folk would write off John Paul as a benefits-sponging user, but Mary distrusted most folk far more than the likes of John Paul. Plus, she knew his grandpa.

'We've met, actually,' said Mary. 'You were a baby. Your grandpa and I used to take you to the duck pond.'

'Yeah?' He tightened his arms, a leg fidgeted.

'He always said you made his life make sense.'

John Paul gulped, brought his legs in a little. 'Were you his probation officer?'

'Not for long.' Joseph was sentenced to twelve months' probation after driving under the influence of alcohol. His daughter, John Paul's mother, had just died in hospital of an overdose. He went to the pub on the way home. Mary had rooted for grandpa in the report she did and helped him get his life together afterwards.

John Paul uncrossed his arms.

'He was impressive, your grandpa.'

He smiled.

Even on shitty weeks like this, one case blowing after another; even with a glamorous suicide, online trolling, and a looming fatal accident inquiry, she was still champion at speed rapport-building. 'Let's have a look at your record, shall we? Usually tells me all I need to know.'

And it did.

Age fourteen, after his grandpa had died, and he was taken into foster care, John Paul needed to drink and vent, thus: assault, breach of the peace (×5), assault to severe injury, assault with offensive weapon (metal toilet-brush holder. According to John Paul it was very offensive).

During his first stint in a secure unit he needed a boost, hence: possession class A, possession class A.

When his dalliance with Charlie turned more serious, he needed money: theft by shoplifting, fraud, reset, theft, attempted housebreaking.

When he lost his phone: police assault.

And when, having just turned twenty-one, he had no friends to steal from or with, as well as requiring a hundred pounds a day himself, and owing Kevin-the-Fucker four hundred for coke he'd been told was free: intent to supply, class A – the index offence for which he would be sentenced tomorrow.

'The indictment says you were in possession of three thousand pounds' worth of cocaine in your freezer.'

'Aye, street value.' John Paul reported that he had agreed to repay Kevin-the-Fucker the four hundred pounds he owed by storing large quantities of the drug in his newly acquired throughcare flat.

'And you decided to put the cocaine in the freezer?'

'Aye, cos me and my mates never use it, ever.'

'In fishfinger packets.'

'Aye, I bought a dozen packets for the gig, cos me and my mates never eat fishfingers.'

John Paul had taken half of the fishfingers out of each of the twenty-four fishfinger packets, and distributed the score bags among them.

'Then I got remanded,' he said. 'And the fridge-freezer was switched off.'

'Why was it switched off?'

'Cos me and my mates never use it.'

Two and a half weeks into his three-week *lie-down*, John Paul's downstairs neighbour phoned the cops to complain about the terrible smell.

'When you think about it, John Paul, which decision do you think landed you in here?' It'd be a difficult choice with so many options, but Mary believed there was always one moment, one conversation, one look, one picking-up-of-a-knife, one drink, one drug, one decision, that changed everything. 'Pick one.'

He thought hard. 'I can't believe I didn't check if the freezer was on.'

Insight: nil.

Offending: escalating.

Risk assessment: very high.

Custody: almost certain.

Mary had written three pages of notes and was now wrapping up. 'Whether you like it or not, I'm going to push very hard for a non-custodial sentence, John Paul. If you keep this shit up, you'll never feel better than you do now, and I know you don't feel good. I'm recommending twelve to eighteen months supervision, with drugs and alcohol counselling as a requirement, potentially a stint in turnaround. There'll be lots of support to help you get work and friends and purpose, and, I've got to warn you, a fair amount of eye contact. I'll put together a good argument when I get back, so you can head off to AA. It's five to eleven now, but don't get up yet. Sit, sit. I need to ask you one last thing before you go, and I need you to stay still, no reaction, when I ask it. I'll keep writing notes as if we're just chatting away about normal stuff like how bad you are at cocaine-dealing. What did you put in my bag?'

'Sorry?'

'About twenty minutes ago, around the time I was writing your name, you slid something into my bag. What is it? Try to look normal. Not too normal!' Mary moved her hand an inch towards her bag, which was on the floor at the end of the table. 'Shall I take a look?'

'It's four grams of cocaine, cut to shit, mind.'

'Oh,' was all she could say, the scenarios forming in her suddenly boiling to a head. None of them made sense; all of them awful.

'I'm sorry,' he said. 'Someone persuaded me to land you in it.'

'Who?'

'No-one.'

'Shall I call Dawn?'

'No, no! My co-pilot, arrived last night.'

'His name Derek McLaverty, by any chance?'

'He's going to give me two more of my own when I get back.'

'Is he? How is that going to work exactly? I'm confused.'

'The plan is I go out before we're finished and tell the officer you tried to give me the stuff.'

'But I was searched on the way in, so they'll know it's from you. In fact, weren't you searched your end? How'd you get it in?' As soon as Mary asked, she realised: in his arse, hence the wriggling. He had somehow managed to retrieve a package from his anus right in front of her, and right in front of the cameras. 'Your excrement is also in my bag?'

He nodded a shame-faced apology. 'I eat healthy in here.'

'John Paul, as ever there are significant flaws in your decision-making processes. The packet is covered in your DNA. You could get a year for this. Did Derek say why? Did he say anything about me?'

'He said you killed his best friend. He said you put him in here, and because of you he might never see his Oskar and Freddie again.'

'Listen, I won't be searched on the way out. Smuggling drugs *out* of prison isn't hard.'

'Really?'

'I can walk out of here with my bag, no problem.'

John Paul was thinking very hard. 'Can I put it back in?'

'Your best plan is to take the package out of my satchel and reinsert it into your anus while chatting to me?'

'Maybe I could snort it, under the table.' He was understandably excited at this idea.

'Tell Derek I said hey.' Mary packed her paperwork into the satchel and covered the small, soiled balloon with a tissue. She stood and shook his hand. 'You look just like him, you know.'

Mary was right. It *was* easy to smuggle drugs out of prison.

She hadn't looked at her phones all morning and wouldn't until she'd emailed John Paul's report. She had to focus, get it done. She managed to get it off in an hour, thanks to a fair amount of copying and pasting.

Getting on with it was the only option in social work. If you stopped getting on with it, you drowned. Mary had been through worse weeks than this. Twelve of her clients had killed themselves on her watch, two of them in the young offender's institution. She'd been ripped to pieces at three fatal accident inquiries, scolded at MAPPA on a monthly basis, torn apart at breach proceedings, sworn at in children's hearings, spat on by angry mothers, followed by desperate probationers, threatened by rapists.

Things had often seemed so horrible that Mary couldn't imagine ever feeling safe again. But disasters blew over in social work. Probably because management didn't have time to deal with this week's disasters. They were only just dealing with last year's.

It was 1.00 p.m. when Mary collapsed on her bed and pressed 'play' on her laptop (*Are We Sluts*, season three, episode six). Her eyes were getting heavy, her legs were getting heavy, her body was becoming part of the bed.

She woke to the intercom buzzing. It was still light, but Mary had no idea what time it was. Before answering, she raced round, looking for somewhere to hide the cocaine. Her decision to put it in her River Island Boot made her wince because it reminded her that she had also hidden a wad of child abuse images in there, probably. She'd never wear those boots again; take them to Oxfam after all this was over. Mary took a breath and answered the intercom.

'Is that Mrs Shields?'

'*Ms.*'

'It's the police, can you let us in please?'

16

Mary expected the police to ask her a lot of questions, but did not expect one of them to be: 'You masturbated to the point of climax while fantasising about Macdowall?' The cop was female, fourteen, and at some point had taken Mary's red notebook from her satchel. Teen cop raised her eyebrows at sidekick cop, who looked busy counting his days to retirement.

Teen cop had already grilled her about Macdowall's death and the hours and days preceding it, and she'd answered with confidence and a fair amount of honesty. Throughout her work life, Mary constantly imagined herself in court, defending whatever she was doing or saying, and was practised at it. Jack used to chide her for this all the time because apparently she applied the rule to everything, including the dishes. The policewoman took notes and, to Mary's surprise, did not seem at all interested in blaming her for Macdowall's suicide or in ruining her reputation and career. In fact, Mary was starting to like teen cop.

'You haven't been online this afternoon?' she asked.

Mary shook her head. 'I was at Lowfield; had an urgent report.'

'Derek McLaverty is using Macdowall's death to promote his cause and sell books. You're the perfect bad gal.'

'He's a bad egg.' Unexpected remark from retirement cop.

'McLaverty was arrested trying to see his kids when he got back from Edinburgh last night. He's safe inside for three weeks, but he's good at ruining lives, even from his cell; he's got a big network. He'll do anything he can to undermine you. Like telling us you had an affair with Macdowall, which is why I'm asking you about your feelings for him. And considering what's written in this notebook, did you?'

'Did I masturbate while fantasising about him, or did I have feelings for him?'

She read out loud: '"Last night I fantasied about Liam Macdowall and pure came like a banshee."'

'I didn't write that, did I? Can I have it back please?' Mary grabbed it and held it tight. She'd burn it tonight. 'On one masturbatory occasion, I thought about Liam Macdowall, but that doesn't mean I had feelings for him, other than work-related ones, most of them very negative.'

'Aren't you married?' asked retirement cop.

'Yes, and over the thirty years I have been, I've masturbated while fantasising about other men approximately twice a week – are you writing this down? You should be writing this down. Therefore – thanks to not being fucked up about sex, thanks to having a healthy relationship with my husband, and also a huge thanks to my vibrators, particularly the Just Ears – highly recommended – I have "pure come like a banshee" to hundreds of men, known and from off the telly. He was a killer, a lifer; he was antisocial, pro-criminal, unemployed and unemployable, alcoholic and a terrible father. I thought about him once, and never again. He's no more important to me than a topless roofer or an inappropriate masseur. He was briefly D list in my hefty and not abnormal wank bank.'

Retirement cop no longer looked dead inside and was taking energetic notes: 'Bunny Ears, you say?'

Teen cop threw her colleague the evil eye.

'*Just* Ears. Great for Mother's Day,' Mary said.

Catherine had left three urgent messages on Mary's Black-berry, the last of which was: *Off to Peterhead. Stay at home and rest. Meeting has been arranged for Mon in office at 4pm, so take it easy and cu then.*

This meeting could take two forms: supervision with Catherine, in her cosy office. Catherine would ask Mary if she was okay, offer her a tissue when she cried about killing her client, reassure her she did not kill him, offer the telephone number of a counsellor specialising in post-traumatic stress disorder, phone her GP and make an urgent appointment. She would resign with immediate effect and they would hug. Mary would hold her head high as she walked to her desk, and everyone would clap because Mary had suffered in this place for thirty years and it was over.

(They'd clap, but they'd hate her guts cos not everyone's got a rich twat husband, do they?)

Or the meeting could be more formal. Fact finding. This would take place in the conference room on the ground floor, with the windows that had never opened, and which smelt of the sweat of neglectful mothers. Present at this meeting would be Catherine, her boss, and maybe her boss's boss. Mary would be terrified, but confident. She was not afraid of the facts. Despite the nature of the meeting, her colleagues would be kind and supportive. She would hand in her resignation and leave quietly by the back door with her head held high-ish.

She fired up her other phone. Facebook and email had gone wild with links to The Lion's Roar and other men's rights sites, all of which portrayed Mary as public enemy number one.

Mary was surprised at how little she gave a fuck. She was too tired to give one. She could have slept for a month. When Roddie's money came in, any day now, she could book a week in a spa, or a month in an American clinic specialising in emotional exhaustion. They'd feed her, force her to eat fruit. She'd get massages and tell people all her shit for a change, bore them with the series of life events that led her to be the most hated woman in Scotland.

Mary turned both phones off again. She must not think about that.

3.00 p.m. What time was Roddie getting in? And how long before she could have a drink: two hours? Unless you're on Australian time of course, which Roddie would be, and which she should maybe try to be on too; so she could selflessly be his jet-lag hag. She poured herself a 'living-room Sangiovese' (smaller in appearance than a 'kitchen' one, but appearances can be deceptive), ran the bath, and took off her clothes. The stress of the last week had taken its toll, and to her delight, she was sporting a significant thigh gap. Mary was looking for the measuring tape when a figure appeared through the frosted glass of the front door. Keys jangled, the door opened. 'Roddie!'

—

They'd always been excellent at long-distance relationships, if the relationship was with each other. Mary had backpacked with a childhood friend the year after they got together, for example – a long-anticipated Asia-inspired experience that ended the childhood friendship. She and Roddie had written to each other each week for six months: happy letters that Mary recently discovered in a biscuit tin and realised were *love* letters.

If anyone asked the secret to their success, they'd both give the same two answers. The first was that they talked. Poor communication was a stupid reason to screw things up, Mary reckoned. So many tragedies could be avoided by a simple conversation, by the quick imparting of relevant information.

Mary was sobbing into his chest. 'Is Jack okay? He's falling for the guy's daughter, we have to stop it.' She didn't want to let him go.

'He's fine, baby. He's absolutely fine. I've been chatting to him.'

'I shouldn't have breached him,' Mary said.

'You should have breached him sooner.'

She held Roddie's face to impart the most important piece of information. 'Derek McLaverty's saying I was having an affair with Macdowall.'

'That's ridiculous.'

'I know.' Mary nuzzled into his chest again, so relieved. 'I have to go to a meeting on Monday about all this. I'm fantasising about resigning then.'

'Yes. Please. Immediately. Go off sick from now till your notice is served; fuck their threats.'

'Have you signed the contract?' she asked.

'Rich is emailing it over tomorrow. And I'll go with you on Monday to make sure you don't chicken out.'

The second secret to their success was that they had fun together. Shit happened, of course it did, but if Mary had something planned with Roddie, she never once wondered if she'd have a good time. It was a given. They both insisted on heavy and regular doses of the stuff, particularly after a period of separation.

'You mean it?' The idea of never going back was too good.

'You are no longer a criminal-justice social worker.'

'I can't abandon my guys without saying anything.'

'Yes, you can. You are never going back. I promise. Never. That's it, done, finito. The rest of your life is about this: us, you and me. From now on, I am the breadwinner. I am an international sensation who's just arrived from an overseas tour, and you know what that means?'

She did know. It meant fun.

'I note we have a bubbled bath.' Roddie said. 'Do we have wine?'

'We have wine.'

'Do we have cannabis?'

'Yes, we have cannabis. Shit, no, I flushed it.' Pause. 'But we do have cocaine.'

Roddie was wearing one of the surgical masks he bought in preparation for the inevitable chaos of the millennium bug. He'd retrieved it from the zombie-apocalypse cupboard in the hall. Mary hoped he didn't notice the canned goods she'd skimmed in the last week for the impromptu food bank she ran from her car boot. She hadn't had time to replace them.

Hands gloved, apron on, he leaned over the first of the three takeaway containers he'd filled with water and decreasing amounts of bleach. With the steady tweezers of a celebrated chin-hair-plucker, Roddie rotated the rubber package, studying the rate at which the chlorinated-water turned brown. When satisfied, he repeated the process in takeaway container two, then three, before placing a pristine-looking balloon on a sheet of kitchen paper and spraying it with disinfectant.

'I can't see any.' Roddie steadied the package with his tweezers, cut the rubber ball with his least favourite knife, and the white powder revealed itself. Their evening was born.

'You think some specks will have seeped in?'

'I'm a hundred percent certain,' said Roddie.

Mary scooped the powder onto a dinner plate and tidied it with her Glasgow Library card. 'Wanna snort some shit?'

Ever since Jack moved out, Mary and Roddie had ordered a gram of Mandy from Johnny each month as a payday treat, and set aside an evening together to dabble in various combinations of the following activities:

Brainstorming business ventures, such as an artist's retreat (Roddie's idea) or the lottery (Mary's).

Brainstorming graphic-novel ideas, such as Menopause Woman (could melt a man with a single hot flush – Roddie's idea), or Misogyny Man (could get fucked – Mary's idea).

Massaging neglected body parts.

Dancing round the kitchen table.

Having the kind of sex they would both swear, on their lives, they'd never had before.

Alas, through no planning of their own, they had taken the wrong drug. That, and perhaps ned excrement, meant neither managed to locate the other's neglected body part nor dance round the table with conviction for any length of time. Mary only managed to complete two of her recently discovered activities – the angry strip, and cooking with resentment. At some point things took an unfortunately serious turn, and Mary told Roddie about Christmas when she was twenty-one and her mum was throwing milk bottles against the kitchen wall, one after the other: *smash*, *smash*, glass all over the floor, and some milk, *smash*. 'Fuck you. Fuck you all.'

Mary had not only said this out loud, she had also done it. There was glass everywhere, and some wine. 'Holy Shit. I'm so sorry. My God, it *is* me. I am the arsehole.'

Roddie walked across the kitchen, glass crunching under the slippers Mary got him for Christmas, and took her hands. 'Don't be daft. It's okay. We shouldn't have taken that coke.'

'I've hit you before.' She was crying.

'You've never scared me. You're unwell sometimes. So am I. I get it.'

'You know what you sound like, Roddie? My victim.'

He held her face and kissed her. 'Mary, you're *tiny*.'

He had melted her. 'That is the nicest thing you've ever said to me,' she said, and burrowed in.

17

Her leg buzzed and a different husband slapped her face. This one's eyes were closer together and had no love in them. 'You told your boss?'

Mary scraped herself upright, taking in the blood on her foot, the piece of glass causing it, the yelling outside, and the time (2.00 p.m.; couldn't be. Where were her glasses?).

There was yelling outside? Their second-floor town flat was in a quiet and leafy part of the inner-city 'village' of Pollokshields and boasted unrivalled views of Maxwell Park. The leg buzz was her phone. She'd fallen asleep on top of it as well as a few other items, including toothpaste and a spoon. 'Told my boss what?'

'That you fantasised about Liam Macdowall.'

Roddie's eyes were on his laptop, thankfully, as she was scared to look at them again. Had her boss, Catherine, leaked this to the press? Surely not. Perhaps it was Retirement Cop.

'Well?'

'I told you about it. It's not a secret. I told you first.'

'Can you not see the difference, Mary? "I told you first", like it was newsworthy. How many other people did you feel the need to inform? You liked the guy, didn't you? Says here you friended him on Facebook. That's not true, is it?'

'What's the noise outside?'

Her attempt to change the subject didn't work.

'Did you friend him?'

'No.'

'No?'

'Not really. I dunno, I pressed a button to keep an eye. "Like" or "join" or something.'

'So, you – whoever you are – friended your client on Face-book and told everyone you fancied him. Right. How much have you been drinking while I've been away?'

'Not much.'

'During the day?'

'No, but I'll be able to now I'm not working.'

'This isn't funny, you idiot.'

Mary's face itched but she dared not scratch.

'A Miss Fiona Bellwood says you answered the phone pissed when Liam called you. According to Miss Bellwood, "Mrs Shields was practically naked and when she answered his call, she screamed: 'Are you fucking someone else?' When she realised Liam was with me, she got angry. She'd been drinking. I could see lingerie and sex tools on her bed." Tell me that's not true.'

'No.' Before today, Mary had lied to Roddie on five occasions, four of which related to not-smoking/smoking, the fifth when she said his attempt at a hipster beard was sexy. She decided not to count this as a lie, as Roddie was not Roddie but a thin guy who hated her.

'Did you fuck someone over there?' She should not have asked, as it made him furious.

'Really? Really, you're asking me that now?'

'Those girls on Facebook, I saw – bet they were all over you, the one with the nose piercing?'

Roddie put his open laptop on Mary's legs and began dressing. 'I'm going to Jack's. Why don't you stay here and relax, perhaps do some light reading?'

Mary glanced at the blog title on the laptop as Roddie slammed the door.

MISANDRIST OF THE MONTH

Goes to Mary Shields, fifty-two, from 20 Mansion House Square, Glasgow. Ms Shields, criminal-justice social worker based in Renfield (pictured above), is the perfect example of everything that's hateful, unfair and ugly in the world. Feel free to disagree in the comments section below but Mzzz Suffradyke, along with her muff mafia are on a mission to ensure female supremacy.

As part of his life licence Menopausal Manhating Mary wouldn't let Liam have a drink, wouldn't let him live in his own home with his daughter, and wouldn't let him touch another woman without asking her permission first. She stalked him, went to his book launch and heckled, turned up at his house at all hours and breached him over the phone minutes before his first major event. She completely failed to consider his needs in her risk assessment, concentrating only the risk he might present to 'known adult females'. How could she have ignored that he intended to kill himself in the river that day ten years ago? That he was suicidal in prison, as he writes in his book *Cuck* (heralded by the *Mail* as 'the most important work on gender to have been published this century'). And yet he left prison without his medication and spent his first days on the outside withdrawing from the antidepressant sertraline while being hounded by a dried-up Clitler. In his pre-release meeting, Sister Shields promised to check with him and his GP about his medication, but she didn't bother. Instead, during his five short days of freedom, she set out to break his balls, and, boy, did she manage that – why else would he tag her in his suicide note? He couldn't bear it anymore. She was just like his crazy wife, Bella, who beat him for years before he cracked. Mary Shields did not want Liam to have a life. She wanted him to feel bad about being a man. I blame her. She killed him.

(Click here to purchase your copy of *Cuck*.)

At least once a year for the last thirty years an official complaint had been made about Mary, each of which required many meetings before it could officially be ignored. She'd been accused of poor time-keeping by a child rapist; Maggie McInnes said Mary locked her in the car and nipped her head for at least three minutes when it was *known* she was agoraphobic; and Rab McCole complained that Mary tried to kiss him and that he said no, which is why she breached him, not cos of, you know, what happened with the fireworks and that.

Complaints didn't scare her. But this was an onslaught, one which had upset her beloved, and she was angry. She hadn't felt so angry since failing at breastfeeding, which is why she was so determined to get everything right after that. Since Roddie left – around 2.20 it was, give or take – she had been overwhelmed with the types of thoughts and feelings she told her guys never to have: thoughts such as what it would feel like to bash Derek McLaverty's head in with a hammer, and feelings such as *excellent*.

The yelling outside was the travelling band of MRA protestors, chanting Mary's worth away. Something smashed against the window. Not large enough to crack it, but loud enough to scare Mary into ringing the police. They told her to call again if she felt significant fear or alarm. Apparently, she was experiencing only a medium level currently. She said thanks and hung up.

Lil and K, who she'd usually be meeting at the pub at 5.00, had left kind messages and would arrive at the house in two hours. She decided to order some food from Bella Brava, which always had what she wanted: 'The antipasti starter, the one with mortadella … Yep, just starter, if that's okay. And three bottles of the house red.' Mary rolled her eyes. 'Okay, so forget the starter and give me as much linguini as it takes.'

A fair amount of pacing took place before the food arrived; the circular kind Bobby Finnigan did in Leverndale after blinding his girlfriend's right eye with a metal pole. There were a lot of metal poles on the streets of Renfield. Knives too; common as dog poo, all the way from Grange Road to Ferntree, many of which unsuspecting eighteen-year-old males tripped over a minute before being stopped by the police. Honestly, the desperate ludicrous stories people told. Mary wished she could transport her fizzing-cold-sore insides to Bobby's ward in Leverndale. It'd be socially acceptable to pace there, and she would do it for as long as the dizziness anaesthetised her.

Roddie wouldn't answer his phone. A banana struck and splattered on the living-room window. Someone shouted – something about Mary. Her head was buzzing. No, it was the buzzer.

'Bella Brava.'

In for four, hold for seven, out for eight. She should write and thank the guy in the yurt. What was his name? In for four, hold for seven, out for eight. She'd have been quite calm when she opened the door if John Paul O'Donnell wasn't standing there.

'You've been doxed.' He handed over the three large Bella Brava bags. 'I got these at the door, saved the guy the trip.'

'I've been what?'

'Doxed. Your address is online.'

'Oh, I've been doxed. Yep, that's me.' Mary almost managed to shut the door, but she'd looked at his face too long. 'I don't do that job anymore. I'm done. In fact, you were my very last report. Please leave me alone. Oh, and I threw it out, John Paul.'

'Sorry?'

'The cocaine. That's why you're here. I threw it out.'

'Yeah, no. Yeah. I got supervision at court. Thanks for the report. I wanted to say that, in person. But, see, yeah, so it's true. I am wondering about the cocaine. If you're not in the job anymore, you're allowed to understand?'

'I threw it out.'

'In your bin, like?'

'Do I need to call the police?'

'I don't think you should. I'll go, don't worry. I'm mad busy; really close to getting a food voucher.'

'Good. Go.'

'Yeah, I'm at step five, about. I rang the Bru and they said to ask my family, but as you know I have no family, so they said to ask my mates and I finally managed to track down Christopher Senior at Kelly-Marie's but he'd been sanctioned the fuck out of, and was on a bender with his mate and his mate's wife Marcie-Anne, as well as her stepdad and Stacey who was going into labour. Pure mayhem, man. So I attended the job centre again and after two hours got a note saying I needed to try the food bank, so I walked three miles to the food bank, and they asked me to get a note off housing or social work saying I'd tried everything and was still hungry, so I walked back to your office in Grange Road and after twenty minutes with the social worker – she was mean, Mary, not like you, fucking cruel, had these tiny little lips, thin and tiny, and this habit of sniffing and at the same time her tongue kinda slithers out and up, a lizard with a cold, but give the lass her dues, after an hour she came back with a note confirming I'm still hungry. So I'm heading to the food bank with that now, in fact I better get a move on.'

'Fuck's sake, come in.' She sat John Paul at the kitchen table and gathered together a care package, which included three of the six main courses of linguine carbonara she'd been forced to buy, as many canned goods as he could carry, and a list of direct telephone numbers, which she was not allowed to give out, including Jo at the job centre, Harry at housing and Bess at RDS. She also gave him all the cash she had – £120.80.

'I promise I won't buy coke with it, and I'll repay you.' John Paul paused. 'Maybe I could start by doing some jobs. Dishes? Or I could take the rubbish out?'

'It's not in my bin, John Paul. And the money's yours. It's none of my business what you do with it.'

Mary always wished she could be a fly on the wall during one of her guys' escapades, like the time Dean McBride fell asleep on the bookie's counter mid-armed robbery. Right now, she was a fly on the window of her second-floor tenement, looking down at John Paul O'Donnell as he rummaged through the small bins in the back drying green. Mary sipped her wine as he contemplated the large bin, stretching on tiptoes and leaning in. His feet left the ground as he reached over, and Mary anticipated what happened next – that his food-filled backpack would tip him further than intended. She chuckled as Glasgow City Council's best swallowed head, arms and torso, the legs wriggling skywards. Mary thought about tossing something at him, but she thought a can of tuna would kill him and she couldn't think what else to throw. Also, Mary's special talent had never been throwing. She was good at spitting, however. At uni, she could spit into Roddie's mouth from six feet. If she was spitting gum or a peanut, her record was nine. She missed those romantic courtship days more than Roddie did.

His legs had stopped wriggling. Perhaps his head was trapped in a bucket. She was about to go down when his legs stretched wide apart and sprung backwards, and he landed on the ground, gymnast style.

Mary opened the window. 'Oi, dickwad. It's not there.'

He did a three-sixty at the hundred or so windows surrounding the pretty courtyard before settling on Mary. 'Mary, doll! No, no, I was just…' Once again, he decided against lying. 'It's really not?'

'It's really not.'

John Paul gave the thumbs-up and scaled a stone wall he need not have scaled, considering the gate was open.

18

K and Lil were best served separately. Every time Mary made the mistake of inviting them both to an event, which she did every six months or so, the night was a disaster. Mary couldn't work out why. Lil had arrived first, bearing typically thoughtful gifts of wine, dairy milk, menthol cigarettes and a trash magazine called *Wizz*. 'The woman on page thirteen has worse boob sweat than you.' Lil always said the sweetest things.

K was panting when she reached the second landing because she was at least fifteen and a half stone. Fifteen and three-quarters, Lil reckoned. There was a spa day riding on who was right, if they could only get it out of her; but after the first attempt to be a girl group went sour (jeans shopping, oops), K advised them that if either skinny bitch ever talked about weight again she would cook them in a pit oven and eat them, bones and all.

They would never talk about weight again, not in front of K, anyhow, so not tonight. K had brought an agenda for tonight, in fact, which involved Mary having a large drink and letting it all out.

'I should have checked about his meds,' she sobbed. 'I didn't give a fuck about him. I screwed up. And now my little boy's getting brainwashed.'

'Shhh, honey. If anything, it's my fault he didn't have his meds,' K said. 'We let him out without, what with all that rigmarole around his book.'

'Shoulda blah, blah,' Lil said. 'Typical female response.

The man made his own decision, and we didn't even know him. Lift your glasses and repeat after me: "It's not my fault.'"

If Mary had to choose between the girls and Roddie, she'd buy Roddie some really nice luggage. He always loved travelling. Apart from anything, she'd have two friends not one, and two is better when your life's being shot at, *poom, poom, poom*, and at 10.08 p.m. via email: *POOM*:

Dear Mary,
I have rewritten the first line of this email many times. Dear Mary sounds idiotic when it's me, Roddie, writing to you, and just Mary comes over angry, which I am, but I don't want to scare you.

I'm at Jack's. I'm reading on Twitter that you slept with Macdowall. I'm looking at a screenshot of you chatting on FaceTime to him. You're wearing my Add It Up t-shirt and your vibrator is on the bed.

I know we need to talk, but I'm not ready. Neither is Jack. He's fine. Holly's very upset, obviously, and helping her is helping him, I think. Anti-feminist girl, feminist boy – might work. Maybe they'll listen to each other.

Looks like the body's being released on Monday. Nothing suspicious, so you're in the clear. Holly wants him cremated that same afternoon – think she's organised it already. I suggest you steer clear of her for now, but my guess is she's going to be around a while.

Roddie
PS: If you Google *Cuck* now, guess whose big, smiley face comes up?

Great friends aren't the ones who are there for you when you've done something impressive – although Mary had never done anything impressive – they're the ones who are there for you when you've done something crap. Lil and K hugged one side of her each and took turns to read the email out loud again, and again – because that's what she needed – analysing punctuation, tone and intent, and deciding on a plan of action, which involved refraining from leaving him further messages and feeling much better after a good night's sleep. Tomorrow she'd find Roddie and Jack, and explain the truths, of which there were many, sadly, as well as the one very effective lie: a quote from Holly Macdowall on the trending The Lion's Roar blog:

'"She seduced Dad on Tuesday night," says orphan Holly. "I visited the next morning and he told me they slept together. He was upset, he seemed scared."'

How could Holly say that? She must have been pressured. Surely they didn't believe this bullshit. To think her boys were both with Holly, listening to lies, and not at home supporting her.

Mary maintenance was a two-woman job, but Lil and K were up for it. Three bottles of Bella Brava later and they were watching *Muriel's Wedding* again, all of them finally numbed.

Mary woke fully dressed and in the recovery position. She sighed. She was supposed to feel better this morning.

One of the many voicemail messages was from Fi, her stand-up teacher:

'Hi Mary, got your message – no worries re missing this week. Attached are some notes on dealing with heckling. PS, I watched the practice set you emailed ... I know I asked you to be bold, but we need a chat about *How Far...*'

Mary could hear the racket outside but decided not to look. She donned her best disguise – one of Jack's hoodies – and put her enormous headphones on, choosing the tune most likely to get her out the door: The Who, 'Red White and Blue'. In front of the full-length kitchen mirror, which she did not look good in for the first time in a while, Mary jumped up and down on the spot while singing '*I love every minute of the day*' – tiny, mad-woman jumps, head hoodied, ears muffed, arms tight by her side. '*I love every minute of the day.*' She grabbed her bag and headed downstairs.

'This isn't on, Mary.' Nora from 1/1. 'I've called the police three times. My bay window's covered in tropical fruit.'

'I'm so sorry. I'll call again too.' Mary pressed the headphones back against her ears and opened the front door. At least twenty people were protesting outside, and it took a moment for Mary to realise that at least half of them were women. Head down like John Paul exiting Glasgow Sheriff Court, she was thankful for the first time that she could never get a park on Mansion House Square.

She drove three blocks to millionaire's row and sparked up Facebook, which was wild with comments regarding the practice comedy set she'd emailed her teacher. Someone had leaked it on social media, and it was everywhere. Mary rocked back and forth as she watched the home video of herself performing into the kitchen mirror with the kind of gusto she only ever had drunk and alone. Egg whisk in hand, Mary alternated between her own accent and – to create the illusion of an audience – a rougher version of the same.

MARY

Who's from Glasgow?

AUDIENCE

Yes, aye, yes, aye, yes!

MARY

Me too! Me too (her lip was quivering). Sorry (she blew her nose), it's the abuse flaring up again. (She paused for an awkward two seconds.) What a buzzkill that fucking me-too thing is though, no? Last night I had a party for my fifty-second – thank you, thank you very much, I am now officially off the market, no longer your competition, ladies, what a relief that is. If I seem interested in your man, it's cause he's a plumber. Lovely evening at mine, seven of us. Hubby's cooked chicken cacciatora, there's polenta, wine, music, anecdotes, some of which were not related to the slow process of dying. It was perfect. That is till Sally pings her glass cos she has an announcement to make. Do you know what it is?

(Another two-second pause.)

Me too! (She put on a whiny voice.) Me too says Sally, and she's crying and she needs a hug from every one of us, including the men, I'm just sayin' – poor guys, they looked nervous. Everyone left after that.

(She paused, and looked at her notes.) Apparently if you send a note to school with your kid just saying 'hashtag me too' your kid'll get away with pretty much anything. My friend Rhona's kid killed a dog in the lane behind the school at lunchtime – he does that a bit – and he got away with it cos his mum wrote a note saying 'hashtag me too'. There were no hashtags in my day. In my day, if you wound up naked on the floor of an old man's bathroom, you kept it to yourself for the rest of your life out of courtesy to absolutely everyone.

(One final pause.)

I'm not saying child abuse is funny! Honey, my second abuser was a very successful comedian, and I still didn't laugh.

Mary opened the car window, tossed her phone in a hedge, then spent five minutes looking for it. She rang K, who didn't answer. She texted Lil, who didn't reply.

They'd probably seen it already. They might hate her. If only they'd pick up. She could totally explain what she meant. She meant good feminist things, she had meant to say – what had she meant to say?

Everyone had started me-tooing. She was shocked by it, to be honest, as she thought she had a secret no-one else had. She thought she had a good reason to be crazy. Turns out every other woman she knew had the same secret, and that she therefore had no excuse for her behaviour. Turns out sex offenders were not 'other', but all around. Perhaps what she meant to say in her set was that they are in this room, they are here, they are us. Should we not let them speak before they act? Where are they to go? Who is a worried teenage boy to talk to? Should we not stop them from jumping off the bridge? That's what she meant, maybe.

Still no reply from K and Lil.

She vomited in a millionaire's hedge.

19

As soon as Jack landed a job, he grew a beard and moved to Finnieston, where resident males were also required to exude an aloofness indicative of complex inner thoughts.

Mary had a spare key, and let herself in. Jack's dog, Marty, greeted her as excitedly as he could, considering she had no treats. Mary missed the hell out of Marty, gorgeous thing.

She assumed the award for Most Disgusting Flatmate would go to the custodian of the green powder that puffed in her face when she poked a (possible) satsuma on the kitchen table, but then she opened Jack's door and was hit by hot, wet air, thick with particles of ejaculate and a Go India hoggie, and she pined for a decayed piece of fruit. Her husband was curled under the covers.

'Roddie! Roddie, come out.'

He pulled at the duvet harder than she did.

'What the fuck, Roddie? You can't believe this shit. Talk to me. This is crazy. I fucked up, but I definitely did not fuck him. Holly's lying. It's Derek, can't you see that? The book is number one on Amazon, you know, so it's working. Don't let his plan work on us, Rodster. Say something. Come out. Sit up. Are you okay? I love you! I love you more than ever. I didn't shag the guy. When I answered Facebook I didn't have my glasses on. I thought it was you. Talk to me. I didn't sleep with him, I didn't.'

Roddie threw his legs over the side of the bed and stared at the wall. 'I don't believe you.'

'Well, I'll convince you. Let me get the kettle on.'

In fact, the grossest-housemate award would go to the person whose baked beans were capped in a glorious mould of deep sky blue. She returned to Jack's sweat pit. 'There's no tea or coffee.'

Roddie was still sitting in the same position, his hand spread out on the bedside table.

'Let me take you home, baby.'

'I want to stay here.'

'Where's Jack?'

'Jack is with Holly.' He still wouldn't look at her.

'She'll be using him to get revenge on me.'

'I think she likes him,' Roddie said.

Mary realised that he was tapping from thumb to pinkie on the bedside table, counting syllables as he spoke: tick, tick, tick, tick, tick; one, two, three, four, five.

'I'm a laughing stock. I am so ashamed.'

When he spoke in fives like this, several bad months might follow. Mary considered her next query carefully, as it was up there with 'Is your period due?' in terms of the anger it might induce. She decided she had to know and that there was no other way to say it:

'Have you taken your meds?'

'Yes, I fucking have.'

Not the answer she hoped for. Medication management would take two days to sort. Never mind, she had all the time in the world, and she would use it all to stop him counting.

She knelt before him and pressed her forehead against his, breathing in through her nose, holding, out through the mouth. Three silent four-seven-eights later and they were breathing in sync.

'When have I ever lied to you? Apart from about the smoking? And the beard?'

Finally, he looked her in the eye. 'You lied about loving anal sex.'

She kissed his hand and then his forehead. 'Every woman lies about that. You smiled. You've forgiven me. And guess what you just said, you just said: "You lied about loving anal sex" – nine syllables. And no-one died. Up, I'm taking you home.'

Mary put on her 'Happy' playlist as they crossed the Squinty Bridge. Somewhere around Ibrox Stadium, Roddie placed his hand on her lap, causing a surge of peace – who knew peace could surge – and it dawned on her that she *had* achieved something exceptional.

With their block in view, as well as the twenty or so men and women on the pavement, Mary knew it was time to say *ciao* to peace for a while. Mary parked some distance away, at the exit to the park. They got out, and she pulled Roddie behind the hedge. 'Before we head over … Do you remember the video I did for stand-up?'

'The Prince Philip one?'

'Christ, no, that was true, but not funny.'

'Rose West?'

'Ha ha! Ha ha. No, the me-too one. I emailed it to Fi for notes. And I guess she must have put it on the internet. What a bitch, doing that.'

'You promised us you'd bin that idea!'

'I know, but last Thursday Fi was going on about being honest and brave and not holding back and taking risks, and on the weekend I was on a real high and alone, and I pressed "send". She should never have posted it without my permission.'

'I bet you'd have given it.'

Mary peeked at her building from the edge of the hedge. The protestors appeared to be quite relaxed – some were even sun-worshipping. A man with a Muff Mafia placard lit the cigarette of a woman holding the lazy end of a No More Patriarchy banner, which may be what sparked the woman on the erect end to screech: 'Abuse isn't funny!' One by one the women rediscovered their anger and joined in: 'Abuse isn't funny!'

The men fidgeted, not quite sure what it would mean if they joined the chant, and what it meant if they didn't.

'You've managed to make the feminists hate you too.' It was Roddie's unwell voice again, flat and not him. He leaned his arm against the hedge.

'I'm not political,' Mary said.

'Afraid you are now.'

The f-word. The idea of being a bad one upset her beyond comprehension. But maybe it was true. She'd always had to lie (at least by omission) to come over as a good one. She said she was anti-marriage, then she got married. She said she'd buy her boy dolls, and she didn't. She said she was happy to be the breadwinner but ruminated about it daily (*home at fucking seven and have to fucking clean and there's no food and I have to cook and the dishes, the dishes, how can you not see there are dishes?*). She said she was delighted for Roddie to sleep in and spend his days with his pencils. She wasn't. She was exhausted, and perhaps as a result she was letting the side down. She was doing everyone's washing every second day, for example, and everyone's dishes two times a day, and everyone's meals three times a day, and watching 'reluctant' porn and having bad thoughts about fat people. Mary had received her grade and it was F.

'I'm a social worker,' she said to Roddie. 'Everyone's always hated me.'

'The thing about you—'

'What's the thing about me?'

'You are a liability, Mary.'

'You do not think that.' Occasionally the multiple-of-five thing seemed to take hold of Mary too.

If Roddie didn't love her, he'd be violating her personal space now. 'You're such a fuck-up,' he said.

'I made a humour miscalculation. It's stand-up comedy. I'm *sorry*. After thirty years in social work maybe I don't understand what's funny anymore.'

'Here we go again.'

'What?' Mary didn't feel like counting out that old argument – about how she moaned, twenty-three years' moaning, making him feel guilty, but refusing to do anything about it, preferring to be a martyr instead – and reverted to defending her cutting-edge comedy. 'Isn't it like saying the n-word if you're black? I'm allowed to tell jokes about child abuse amn't I?'

Roddie put his hands on her shoulders and leaned her into the hedge. 'There *are* no jokes about child abuse.'

'That's nine syllables.'

'Chi-ld, *chi-ld* – two, that adds up to ten.' Roddie consolidated his shoulder-hold as well as the hate in his eyes. She'd lost him again: the second time in years, both times today, and she would not have it.

'So I should have posted "me too"? I nearly did one night because I couldn't remember how to play solitaire and I couldn't work out why I *wouldn't* post it, then I imagined myself three hours hence, hovering over the laptop on my fourth kitchen Sangiovese and at last, someone likes it. John

Anderson. Who's John Anderson, I wonder? Lil's partner's unemployed actor brother who lives in London with a cat he says he loves but is killing with too much fresh tuna. And maybe after three hours like that, hovering, nine people I don't know will have liked the story I told, names and all. Because, if I'm gonna do it, I said to myself earlier, then I'm gonna do it. Brother Kevin Smith, I posted. Mr Ronald Kinnaird, I told the world. And I told the world about the cold lino of the gymnasium floor, and the cold ceramic of the bathroom floor, because they were on my mind for a moment thanks to hashtag me too. And so there I am hours later, me and my nine likes, pacing the flat wondering how to reply to inevitable messages from cold-floor children, hundreds of them by now, probably: why didn't you tell someone about Brother Kevin, Mary? Why didn't you save me?'

'Will you just fuck off!' At some point Roddie had let go of her shoulders. He was now yelling at the two women at the park's exit.

'My niece was raped,' said the smaller of the two.

'Did you ask your niece if you could tell two complete strangers that?' Mary said.

The smaller woman – thirteen-and-a-half stone, Mary reckoned, but she was prone to underestimation – looked to her far-larger pal for help. After some headache-inducing staring it became obvious that her pal didn't understand anything about anything, leaving Smaller Woman to think on her feet, which she was not good at standing on, let alone while thinking.

'You should be ashamed of yourself,' she said to Mary.

Roddie's mission was probably the same as Mary's at that moment – to get across the road, inside, and lock, lock,

lock. But somewhere between the lane and number twenty, a twenty-metre diagonal journey at most, their missions diverged in a very unlikely way.

20

TO: Procurator Fiscal's Office, Glasgow
FROM: Mary Shields
SUBJECT: Roderick Lawson

My husband of thirty years, Roderick Lawson, was remanded in HMP Lowfield this afternoon, having been charged with assault (domestic). He will appear in Glasgow Sheriff custody court on Monday and intends to plead not guilty. I am writing to explain the unusual circumstances surrounding the incident, to assure you that I am in no way his victim, and to vouch for his good character.

At approximately 2.00 p.m. this afternoon, Roderick (Roddie) and I arrived at Mansion House Square after visiting our son in Finnieston. Approximately twenty people had taken up position at our front door and began taunting us as we attempted to go inside.

Around ten male protestors had arrived on our doorstep the previous afternoon in response to the suicide of Liam Macdowall, whose life licence I supervised. Macdowall's book, Cuck, Letters to My Dead Wife, *had catapulted him to cult status among men's rights activists. The male protestors were at my house because they blamed me for Macdowall's death. This was due to a vicious hate campaign against me by Derek McLaverty. On his blog,* The Lion's Roar, *he published many false accusations about me, the most relevant at this point that I had been having an affair with my life licensee.*

My husband had arrived home from a business trip to Australia two days prior to his arrest. He was jet-lagged and very upset that I was being trolled online, and that he was being ridiculed and belittled as a cuckold, or 'cuck' as the men's rights activists and the alt-right were calling him. Roddie and I have a healthy and happy relationship. I did not have an affair with Liam Macdowall. Roddie knows I did not have an affair with Liam Macdowall.

When Roddie and I returned home around 2.00 p.m. this afternoon, ten women or thereabouts had joined the protest at Mansion House Square. This was in response to a practice stand-up comedy video I emailed to my night-class teacher for feedback, which I assume she leaked without my permission.

Feeling a very high level of fear and alarm, Roddie and I phoned the police and then attempted to gain entry to our close. When the protestors blocked our entrance, I asked them for a chance to explain myself, and eventually they agreed to listen. I apologised to anyone who was upset by the very rough private-practice video I wish I'd never done and which I now understood was in bad taste and not funny. I told them how sorry I was that Liam Macdowall had taken his own life. I asked that they please give way so my husband and I could go inside. The crowd parted, but as we were about to close the door, one of the men yelled, 'What kind of man are you?' By the time Roddie reached the fourth step, the men were chanting 'Cuck! Cuck! Cuck!' and this is when the incident occurred.

I was on the step below my husband when he stopped and turned around. I placed one of my arms on the bannister and the other against the wall to prevent him from going outside, which, by this time, was what he wanted to do. Sirens added to the chaos, as well as one of the men banging on the glass while shouting: 'She has taken your balls, man.'

Roddie had no intention of hitting me. I have attached a photograph taken by one of the agitators outside, which you can find on Twitter using #getthebitch. In this photograph you will see Roddie's elbow is an inch away from connecting with my face, a collision which resulted in his arrest and the loss of half of one of my teeth. I can confirm that the impact occurred because I barricaded him. If you zoom in on Roddie's face, you will see he looks angry. This is because the men are still yelling 'cuck' and I'm refusing to move, which is an unhealthy relationship behaviour, and which incited the men outside to bang on the door and yell, 'Get the bitch. Get the bitch. Cuck. Cuck. Cuck!' and which caused my husband to lunge forwards in a spontaneous manner.

I ask you to now zoom in on my face. An elbow's about to knock my tooth out. What do you see in my expression? Do I look afraid? In instances such as this, fear is an honest measure, is it not? I have worked as a criminal-justice social worker for thirty years. Many of my clients have been guilty of hitting their wives or partners, and I have read hundreds of letters like this, which I admit I have disregarded, seeing them as evidence that the victim continues to be manipulated by their abuser. I have often wished I was a fly on the wall at the time of my service users' offences. Well in this case I was, and you can be too if you zoom in on my face. At the moment of contact, I was not afraid of my husband. I look aggressive, do I not? I am not afraid of Roddie. He has never hit me or scared me in any way.

Yours faithfully,

MARY SHEILDS
LLB DIPSW MSW

NB: I have cc'd my husband's lawyer, Adeela Hamdani, into this letter.

NB2: As an accredited user of the LC/SMI risk assessment tool, I can confirm that Mr Roderick Lawson has a MINIMAL level of risk and need factors in relation to offending.

21

Am I mad?

Apparently, a mad woman would not ask this, but Mary didn't rate 'apparently'.

'Apparently' was Thomas McInnes telling Gregor Thom that Mary Shields sucked off Johnny Simpson three times by the loch, and anyway, Mary had firm evidence that she was – self-awareness notwithstanding – a card-carrying, attic-worthy, lunatic.

The first piece of evidence was the email she sent to the Procurator Fiscal. Rather than applying the twenty-four-hour calm-yourself rule, she had pressed 'send' as angrily as each of the letters preceding it, and now realised this could jeopardise Roddie's defence.

I should have sent this to you first – oops, Mary messaged Adeela, a mutual pal from uni and a hot-shot defence lawyer.

OMG Mary, Adeela replied. *Write to no-one, speak to no-one. Stay home till after court on Monday – two more sleeps. Don't even talk to Jack. Talk to NO-ONE.*

The second piece of evidence of mental incapacity was that Mary was having auditory hallucinations. Since arriving home from the police station she'd been hearing an orchestra that simply could not be real. She could hear it very clearly with the shutters closed, with all the appliances off, sitting cross-legged, in the hallway. The shutters didn't block out all the never-ending evening sun, and pincers danced on the floor around Mary to the orchestra that was definitely playing.

Madness, of course, that an orchestra was playing, but Mary could hear bagpipes, and drums, as well as track-laughter that seemed to ridicule the ruined pieces of her, one of which she held in her hand.

Roddie might be writing her a letter in B hall now, in which she's the abuser. For example: *Dear Mary, Derek suggested I record a memory. This is my memory of the most recent time. You are standing in the kitchen smashing glasses. Your eyes are dim. I can't find you in them. 'Fuck you all!' You smash another, and a piece of glass hits my shin.*

The pipe band passed by – it was a pipe band! Not madness. The 12th July was approaching, and the Orange Order was already flexing its muscles in this largely Asian neighbourhood. Mary wondered if racist Simon Gallacher would be drumming along.

She wasn't hallucinating. It was a pipe band.

And the laughter was coming from downstairs. Nora in 1/1 must be having a dinner party. Mary didn't get invited after the fourth time, because she hated cooking and didn't reciprocate. She suggested paying for a takeaway, but this was offensive to Nora. There were all sorts of rules. Shame, Nora made great lamb.

Mary dragged herself to the bathroom. Adeela was right, she should stay inside until court on Monday – two sleeps. She shouldn't talk to Jack, should not leave the flat. She opened her mouth for the first time since being questioned at the station and beheld the one big problem with this plan.

Her tooth.

On her palm was one jagged half of her left front tooth, smashed by the elbow of her beloved. She'd found it, thankfully, with the help of the feminists, who suddenly liked her again cos she was bleeding. She couldn't turn up at court looking like this – and *this* did not look good. The toothlessness aged her by thirty years and would add a further thirty months to Roddie's sentence if found guilty.

Mary superglued her tooth in front of the bathroom mirror. She held her mouth wide open and fanned her teeth for sixty cat-dog seconds, then checked her dental work. Her left tooth was very clearly in two pieces, which very clearly did not quite match. She yanked at her Picasso tooth-work, but the glued piece wouldn't come out. Fuck.

She phoned Bella Brava and ordered seven bottles of wine and ten portions of cold lasagne.

Wine – yep.

'Rescue' playlist – tick.

House cleaned – tick.

Bath – done.

Clean sheets, candles, and a sad sneeze of a wank – tick.

1.00 p.m., and Mary had done everything she could to stop the itching. *Sex and The City: The Movie* didn't help, *even* the wedding dress shoot. Bella Brava red wasn't working either, but she decided to try harder.

The moisturiser burned her scratched calves, and she used it as an excuse to scratch again. She had to clear her head, make an action plan and fix this. Fuck it, everything can be fixed, even thoughts, allegedly, if you have a flipchart.

Mary had three under Jack's bed. She'd thought about stealing them from work but had in fact ordered them online, because she loved them and had naively always hoped for a moment like this. She assembled the flipchart with a lot of heavy breathing then couldn't remember why she'd done it, jumping wholeheartedly into an alternative and excellent reason for the flipchart being there:

<u>REASONS TO LIVE</u>

Mary wished she hadn't worded it exactly that way, it's not what she meant, and she shouldn't have used red felt-tip and capitals and underlined it. It looked suicidal and she wasn't. Granted, she'd been thinking about death a great deal: of the different ways it might happen. And she'd accidentally tunnelled into a Netflix sub-genre about creative people, such as poets and painters, who have lots of fun then kill themselves. Once, after re-watching *The Hours*, she got in the car and drove to Troon beach. She removed her shoes and socks and walked on the wet sand until her toes reached the water. It was bloody freezing.

She was not suicidal, unless she could scratch herself to death, which, right enough, Liam Macdowall practically did in the end, but Mary wasn't wanting to do that. She ripped the page from the flipchart and burned it in the log fire she must have lit a while back. The flame ignited the reason for the flipchart. She was going to fix everything, which meant making an action plan. Mary loved action plans so much. The examining of a life in crisis, the defining and dividing of a problem, the promises you make to try and improve things. Mary chose the blue pen. She didn't underline or use capitals. Her question was unintimidating:

What is the problem?

There were too many problems. Mary had filled three pages with them and was now howling to a song she should not be playing on repeat. *'This too shall pass'*, the lyric promised,

'This too shall pass'. It usually helped, but the pipe band would not be beaten by acoustic therapy, and her situation was more serious than late-night shame or early-morning hopelessness, and was not passing.

She ripped the pages from the flipchart and changed the question to:

Who is the problem?

Her first answer deserved to be in red and in capitals and underlined:

ME

If Mary was being interviewed for a court report, she'd be talking about her childhood now, relaying that she was sexually abused twice before the age of five – two one-off occasions thankfully, but damaging nonetheless. She'd be speaking about her parents' response, which was fantastic. They did everything right, which is probably why it never happened again, and why Mary had a very happy life and marriage, till today. She'd be confessing that her mother smashed bottles against the wall one Christmas, but that she only did this once and cleaned it up immediately. Mary was twenty-one at the time. Come to think of it, her mum was around Mary's age when the smashing happened and would later refer to this period as her 'difficult time'. She became moody and tired. She left her job. And she moved to Spain with Mary's dad, leaving Mary to graduate, start her terrifying career, get married and have a child completely alone. Being abandoned at twenty-one isn't a thing, though, so Mary had never dared complain about it; but she and Roddie made a pact never to abandon Jack.

Mary yearned to ring her mum, to hear her say: 'Harry, it's Mair!'

She longed to hear her dad clapping in the background: 'My baby girl!'

She and her boys had wonderful summers in Spain. Hopefully they'd get back in the habit again. Her parents were in their eighties now, and Mary didn't want to infect them with her worries. She dialled but hung up before it was connected.

Even with good parents, you're fucked, Mary thought. *Imagine how screwed up Jack could still turn out to be.* She was sobbing the way Jack used to when he was little – no holding back. He stopped the howling over a decade ago, but he was always up for a hug. She was proud she knew a man who hugged and cooked and danced, and that she got him to adulthood without being forced into a white van.

She turned off the song, threw her latest flipchart attempt in the fire, and reconsidered the question.

Who is the problem?

Beckoning the power of Lil, she decided not to take the blame and wrote another option. After she'd written the name, she imagined the ghost of her inner social worker levitating above her, all black and smoky, and with pleading eyes – *Please let me come back.*

'Fuck off,' Mary said to the apparition before underlining the correct answer to *Who is the problem?*

DEREK McLAVERTY

Mary's nest seemed to be trembling. She wandered from room to room in search of a stable piece of ground. She'd have to move from here because of Derek McLaverty. He'd managed to destroy her life in less than a week, and there was no sign of him stopping. <u>DEREK McLAVERTY</u>, he was the problem, and Mary would fix him.

How? She knew better than to fight back online. She didn't even know what Whatsup was. And she didn't want to kill him, as this would mean losing the moral high ground. *What matters to him?* she wrote on the chart. *His kids?* (obv not). *His ex-wife?* (nah). *How do you bring a man like him down?*

It was getting dark at last. The Orange men had disbanded, and Mary felt safe enough to open the kitchen window for some air.

A bin clanged. Someone was standing out the back. Mary grabbed her keys, headed downstairs and unlocked the door to the garden. 'John Paul?' She could see the shape of him standing there, the cheeky bugger. 'John Paul, I told you it's not in there.'

He didn't move or say anything.

Mary lit the ground with her phone as she walked across the green. 'Are you hungry? I've got lasagne.' She could do with some company, and John Paul was the only person in the universe who didn't hate her guts. 'Come on, I'll feed you.' Her phone-light reached his feet. She lifted it to illuminate his face.

Jimmy McKinley's face.

'Jesus Christ. What the hell are you doing here?'

'Where is it?' said her elderly sex offender.

'I don't know what you're talking about.' At first Mary meant what she said, then it slowly began to dawn on her.

'Do you know how many years I worked on that?'

'Worked on what, Jimmy? I'm calling 999.'

'Where is it?'

'Police thanks ... this is Mary Shields of 20 Mansion

House Square.' Mary hadn't really dialled, she was speaking to herself. But it did the job. Jimmy backed off and hobbled out of the gate.

When she opened the back door to enter the close, Nora from 1/1 was waiting, steely faced. 'This is out of order, Mary. We're having a meeting tomorrow. It can't go on.'

'What time?' She was running up the stairs; didn't have time for this crap.

'You're not invited,' said Nora. 'It's ABOUT YOU.'

She was out of breath as she grabbed her River Island boot from the drawer under the bed. How could she have forgotten? She had to ring Minnie at the OMU, tell her what she'd found. Where was her work-issue Blackberry? Not in her bag, not on the kitchen table, not in her coat pocket. It was in the living room, on the chair, and if she hadn't been standing in front of the flipchart when she dialled Minnie's number, she may not have had an epiphany.

What is important to a man like Derek McLaverty?

She stared at the flipchart as Detective Sergeant Minnie Johnstone's phone rang out.

How do you bring a man like him down?

One of his blog comments was echoing in her brain: 'Even her cuck husband and beta son hate her guts #getthebitch #getthebitch, #getthebitch, #getthebitch.'

Mary hung up and shook her River Island boot. She knew how.

The pen drive.

PART THREE

THE PAEDOPHILE

22

At 4.00 a.m. Mary donned one of the wigs she sometimes wore for Roddie, turned on her 'Riot Grrrl' playlist, and walked over to Shawlands. As always, she waved as she passed the street she grew up on. When she was a kid, her red-sandstone terrace had seemed an eternity away from the tenements and mansions of her current multicultural hood. It was, in fact, one hundred metres. Liam Macdowall's flat was another hundred, and she was walking it alone, reading what happened here a few hours earlier: in chips and curry sauce, in overflowing outdoor ashtrays, and in an abandoned shopping trolley filled with loose red apples. Mary, like most Glaswegians, had tried living in sunny places, then returned to Glasgow because it was better than everywhere else.

It was pissing down.

Her dad had pushed her on the swings across the way. She changed the playlist to 'Happy' and turned it down a notch. Thirty years later she'd done the same for Jack, who always looked miserable mid-flight. It shocked her when he yelled 'Higher!' because his chubby face was saying, *I am about to die*. He had many, many fears, and at the age of five had already resolved to conquer them all.

The Shed nightclub was to her left. Mary first hurled there, just before her first kiss, which was beside the Co-op. She and Darren O'Donohue were into each other for a while, despite the vomit snog, but his family moved to Canada to feel more joy. Darren had menopause boobs now, too.

She'd proposed to Roddie at the Granary, which was to the right. Not proposed so much as apologised for a girly weakness and suggested a show of hands.

Nostalgia was making Mary lose revenge-momentum. She put her hand up to block out the karaoke pub she and Roddie frequented in their early forties, and the organic grocer's she and Roddie decided to frequent in their twenties but never did. They should. If they made it through this, they should buy their veg from there. And they should eat veg.

Mary pressed the service buzzer, not expecting the door to open at this time of night. Thankfully it did, because plan B was to scale the back wall, creep across the green and check the back door, and if that was locked she didn't have a plan C. By the time she knelt by the small pot plant on Liam Macdowall's landing, she'd forgotten why she was at a dead client's flat, in the middle of the night, suffocating a pen drive with her palm.

The device had become very hot. She didn't want to look at it, but she couldn't let it go.

Even if she put it in her pocket it'd be better, but she couldn't. She might well know someone on it. Renfield had exploded a century or so ago, and the shards of its population of weavers had since whirled around the area, colliding, exploding again. There was no such thing as serendipity in Renfield, because seemingly chance events were never beneficial. There was no synchronicity here either, because events were never meaningful, no matter how many you had in a row. Good people had lived good lives here, and their descendants were doing five-hour shifts to get a food voucher. Faces swirled before her, of the children she'd known over the years. Vanny could be on the pen drive. How often did her mother leave her alone? How many foster carers did she have? Christopher Senior might well be on it, although he'd have been Christopher Junior then. Maybe even Mary herself was on there. If it was a lifetime's work, it wasn't out of the question. Mary shook herself. She couldn't remember a camera on either cold-floor occasion, but she couldn't remember much at all really, other than genital stimulation, to her shame.

Macdowall's key wasn't under the pot plant, as it had been when she last visited. She checked under the mat, and on the ledge above the door. She pushed the letterbox open and with her fingers separated the fibres of the brush strip. She could see the dining table under the window, which still had Derek McLaverty's silver MacBook on it. Neither resident had returned home after the Edinburgh Book Festival. One was dead, one was in jail. Nothing had been moved since Mary was here; or so it seemed.

She found herself surveying the joint for a break-in – i.e., she looked at the locks on the front door. Two, that was all. Menopausal Mary had kicked the authors' toilet cubicle with great aplomb – she was one of those women others admired, but no-one was reporting about that. It'd be Misandrist Mary who'd send this door flying because right now Mary couldn't think of one good reason not to hate men.

The pen drive was sizzling. She needed to sit down.

Mary was in Pollok Park now, but it'd taken a while to get there. She'd staggered from Liam Macdowall's doormat, down the stairs, and run all the way along Pollokshaws Road to the park entrance. Once inside, she'd tossed the pen drive in a bin, which she regretted immediately, particularly when she realised it was a dog-poo bin, filled with badly tied black bags leaking wet turds. She put her head inside to retrieve it because she had to give it to the police, but a woman in heels and a small dress suddenly appeared from the dark green of a woodland walk. The woman's blonde hair was dishevelled; her ankles at constant risk of breaking as her heels sunk into the muddy path.

'Are you okay?' Mary didn't have her phone, but she could get across the road and dial 999 in ten seconds. Her first aid was out of date, but she'd give it a whirl. She had some cash in her pocket if that's what was needed, and she knew a local taxi firm's number by heart.

'Me! Aye. Why?'

'Just thought I should ask.'

The woman grimaced. 'Should I ask you why you're wearing a wig with dog shit on it?'

The question was fair enough.

When Mary examined her palm at the lights, she felt certain the pen drive had left a mark. She chose a new playlist: 'Everything's OK!'

Roddie would get out tomorrow.

Derek McLaverty would find a new woman to hate.

Jack would forgive her for all the things she'd done wrong.

She was light and fast all the way home. Thank God she'd come to her senses in time.

Planting abusive images on Derek McLaverty's laptop! What was she thinking?

23

Revenge fantasies are like warts. You don't choose them; you hate them, and you pick at them to make them go away – but you'd miss the picking if they did. Mary had been picking hers since 10.00 a.m.

How could she not look online? How can jurors not look? Everyone always looks.

She held out till 10.00, which was a good few hours after her trip to Pollok Park. She was proud of herself, and tipsy again, but what else was there to do but drink and sing and have a bath and go online?

She only looked for a few seconds, but it was long enough. Blogs and tweets and posts and messages had divided the problem of Mary into parts: feminist, wife, mother, social worker. Crazy rants, but everyone seemed to agree on one thing – Mary was *bad* at all of the above. Derek McLaverty was doing an excellent job of destroying her from his cell. She imagined him inside, posting from his illegal phone, recruiting vulnerable men in AA meetings – maybe even Roddie. He'd already managed with Jack, after all.

She deactivated her Facebook account and closed her email address. She ripped the SIM from her personal mobile, stomped on it and threw it out the kitchen window. She put her laptop in the drawer under her bed, cut the power cord and threw it away. She grabbed her work satchel and tossed her diary on the fire. She ripped up her interview notes and watched them burn: *Goodbye Bradley the Perv. Farewell Simon the Racist. Ta-ta Sad Jamie – hope you get the right meds. Ciao*

Jason the Stalker, Robert the Rapist, Kieran the Homophobe, Sam the Schizophrenic, John Paul the Ned.

For some reason, she couldn't ditch her work-issue Blackberry, nor burn John Paul the Ned. She'd miss the likes of him. She'd miss asking questions she'd never have the gall to ask her son. She'd miss getting answers.

Mary was desperate to hear Jack's voice, but she was terrified what it might sound like. It might sound like a man who wasn't on her side.

She was howling over family photo albums, which Jack had spent weeks organising last summer. (She paid him eight pounds an hour.) There was one for every three years of his life. No-one would know how scared Mary was when she brought him home, not by the pictures in album one anyway. She looked happy and confident feeding him in bed, kissing his head. There was a hint of her worries in the book on the bedside table: *How to Bring up Boys*, but you'd have to zoom in to know that. Mary didn't let on how terrified she was of getting it wrong.

Aw, there was Jack in bed, age about seven, his dad sitting beside him, telling him 'facts', as he did every night for years. As a result of this ritual, Jack could now win any quiz in town. While the delivery changed, Roddie and Jack had continued swapping facts ever since. The two of them never stopped talking. Arguing. When Mary tried to join in, she regretted it. She knew nothing about Catalonia or utilitarianism.

In the sixth album, Jack was making a Malaysian banquet for Christmas dinner. Perhaps wrongly, she had viewed his love of cooking as a sign that she had got it right.

Jack might not be on her side anymore. He might hate her. He might be roaring that his mother ruined him, that it was his mother's fault; she was the reason.

How could that be?

She began picking at her wart.

The key's under the mat, Mary imagined. *I tip-toe in, download the pen drive onto McLaverty's laptop and leave.*

The key's under the mat. I am wearing a trench coat. I walk in, download the pen drive, and leave.

The key's not under the mat. I kick the door in with my River Island boot. They've found their place with the trench coat. Always knew they would. I walk in, download the pen drive, leave the door snubbed open and exit. Later that night, I don a disguise, walk somewhere random and make an anonymous call to the police with the disposable mobile I've bought. The husky voice I use totally works with the outfit. I throw the mobile away and head home, smiling, because I have stopped Derek McLaverty. In bed I imagine Derek McLaverty being escorted to the sex-offender's unit in Lowfield. He is the lowest of the low. A work squad passes in the quadrangle, and someone calls him a beast, another guy spits on him. One day soon, a rapist or a wife-beater will kick the shit out of him to gain status, as advised by Liam Macdowall in his book Cuck. *When he gets out, someone like me will stop him from seeing his kids, going to the pool, having a dog, getting a job, taking a holiday, being online: you must not, you must not; you will not, you will not. Someone like me will approve his ground-floor unfurnished flat on a ghost estate ruled by vigilantes, and someone like me will spring visits on him to check how often he wanks and what he thinks about when he comes. He'll be forced to do groupwork with the other registered sex offenders, and even those guys will hate him; even the guy who raped his granddaughter will feel superior because McLaverty's a Denier and everyone hates a Denier.*

The key's not under the mat. I use a paperclip to unpick the lock because I am very good at that, but the neighbour hears me and calls the police. The police officer is called Callum Hendrick. He has strong arms and is checking out at my breasts...

...Three minutes later...

The key's not under the mat, and I do not know for certain how to download a pen drive onto a MacBook or how a MacBook works even.

Intrusive thoughts.

Mary phoned a taxi. She needed to see her husband.

By the time she was inside the rotating glass doors of Lowfield, she felt certain she'd pass as sober in reception. (She wouldn't have a lengthy driveway ago.)

'Hey Davie.' Davie had been an officer for more than thirty years. He was one of the gooduns in Mary's opinion, but in Mary's opinion he was also a prick.

'Which bad boy brings you here on a Sunday morning?' he said. 'Shouldn't you be at St Patrick's?'

'You know me, Davie boy, I'd rather go to a mass shooting than to Mass.' Mary had decided halfway up the drive that she wanted to see Roddie in agent's, where they'd have their own room to talk; where there'd be no prisoners eyeing them. To ensure this, she needed to pretend her husband was a client. 'Um it's Roderick Lawson. He's on remand.'

Davie checked his antiquated paperwork. 'You didn't book this, Mary?'

'Did I not? Oh my God, it's the menopause.' Mary loved

telling men ovary-related stories. 'I keep forgetting things, losing things. You watching the Winter Olympics?' She changed the subject.

'Aye with the grandweans, the curling anyway.' Davie's tone indicated that he either hated curling and his grand-kids, or that he was from Fife.

'Did you see the paired figure skating? German, whatsh-ername. Wow. The bladder control. There'd be a wet patch on my fanny every twirl.'

Davie had gone pale and was phoning the remand hall. 'Roderick Lawson. Can you bring him over immediately? It's his social worker.'

After she was scanned, Mary put her shoes and belt back on and took a seat in the waiting area. She'd been in this halfway room on hundreds of occasions and always used the time to read records, case notes, and any previous reports, so she knew the score before she met the guy, unless he was a first-timer like Roddie. If she was doing Roddie's court report, she'd have to start from scratch. The ones she started from scratch were always the most satisfying.

At last the door opened, but the wrong door. It was Davie from the foyer area, which was almost the real world. He looked mad.

'Roderick Lawson is your husband…'

Mary gasped at the revelation. 'Fucking menopause.'

A few minutes later, Mary was sitting in the governor's office. Luckily, Karen was on duty.

When she came in, she closed the door and gave Mary a huge hug. 'Week from hell, eh?'

'It's certainly in the top three,' said Mary. 'How's Roddie, is he okay? Can you check he's got his OCD meds? Paroxetine, fifty milligrams, once a day.'

'I already checked, and don't worry, he has. We're kinda thorough about that right now.' Karen handed Mary a tissue. 'Your mascara's running.'

She was drenched. When she wiped her face, the tissue turned into a rainbow of wet, stale makeup. She sighed – imagine having spare energy to fix her face. 'He's nowhere near McLaverty, is he?'

'Same hall I'm afraid, but no contact.' K poured a glass of water, put a Berocca in it, and handed it to Mary.

'Can you keep it that way?'

'I'll do my best. Drink it.'

Mary downed the vitamins as directed. 'I'm a bad feminist.'

'Ha, join the club,' Karen said. 'I watched *Tess* again last night. Nastassja Kinski fix. Can't help myself. The guy makes great films. Should we run away to Goa, Mair? Get away from all this toxic bullshit?'

'Goa. The tickets are on me. I think Lil hates me. I haven't heard from her.'

K began removing and reapplying Mary's makeup. 'That's because her own me-too disclosure was a really big thing, if you remember. You need to think more than you drink.'

'I know, I know.'

'Why would you want to help them weaponise it, for fuck's sake?'

'I don't! I didn't mean to.'

'Apologise to Lil, and quit stand-up, obviously. You're about as funny as a crèche in D Hall.' K checked Mary over, then dabbed some water on her hair in order to flatten a stray lump. 'Listen, Roddie doesn't want to see you.'

'What? Why? Ouch.' K was yanking her hair; it wouldn't stay put.

'Because they pulled out of the deal. He's very upset. Ah, there.'

Phew, the makeover was over. 'What deal?' All sorts of scenarios raced through Mary's head, most of them court-related and ending in a lengthy prison sentence.

'You haven't heard? The graphic novel – the publisher pulled out of the contract. Difference in value base; something about a code of conduct.'

She felt sick. Eighty K, most of which she'd spent in her head, no longer. Roddie had worked for years on spec, i.e., unpaid, and thought he'd finally made it.

He'd be counting in fives for the rest of his life.

And she wouldn't be able to leave work, she'd have to go back to that place till she was sixty-eight and had one polyp per disappointment. So selfish to think about herself.

'What value base?' she asked.

'Either it's because Roddie's a wife-beater,' K said, 'or it's because he's got a wife they wanna beat.'

It was Dawn, the officer on duty when she first interviewed John Paul, who escorted Mary from the governor's office, through admin, and back down to the agent's area. Mary was already furious, red-mist furious in fact, when they arrived in agent's, but as she began walking past the glass-windowed interview rooms, her rage became uncontainable, her nose-breathing loud enough for Dawn to say:

'You okay?'

As they passed interview room eight, she said 'Aye,' but

it wasn't true, and it became less so when Mary glanced in room seven.

Derek McLaverty was sitting in room seven. His face caused Mary's face to explode, the way Renfield did around a century ago. She could feel its severed parts smashing against each other, an eye against a nose, broken tooth against lip, and before she knew it she'd opened the door and barged in.

'Get the fuck out of my life,' she said.

'Excuse me?' Even in prison garb McLaverty managed to look superior.

'You do someone a favour to get your polo shirt ironed?' Mary was disappointed in everything she'd said so far. Her brain was too muddy and her head too hot to be a grown up. The more she looked at Derek, the more he morphed into Tommy McInness, who bullied her at school. Toxic Tommy. Dickwad Derek. All the same.

'You have a problem with grooming?' Derek was scanning her matted hair, her broken tooth (she closed her mouth) and the sleeve of her shirt, which was the colour of Sangiovese.

McLaverty's lawyer, dressed in weekend wear of designer jeans and a black t-shirt, turned to protest: 'Hey, get her out of here. Dawn! Dawn?'

If Dawn was trying to get Mary out, she didn't notice.

Derek's pose was determinedly relaxed: foot on knee, elbow on back of chair.

'You talked to your mate, didn't you?' she said.

'Which mate?'

'Rich, RG Books, I saw him chatting on your Cuck Facebook page earlier today. You've ruined my husband's career out of pure badness.'

Dawn put her hand on Mary's arm; she flicked it away.

'And you used a vulnerable young boy to try and harm me, right here, in one of these rooms.'

'Are you feeling all right, Mary? Having a hot flush?' Derek smiled.

Mary lunged forward, but Dawn grabbed her arm and pulled her back.

'Get out of here,' the usually flamboyant lawyer said. He packed less punch in jeans.

Being pulled from the room didn't stop Mary's rant: 'You lied about me having an affair, you branded my husband a cuckold. You've destroyed him, you fucking arsehole. You get out of my husband's life, and you get your claws out of my son.'

'Tell you what, Mary, I'll get my claws out of yours if you get your claws out of mine.'

Mary broke free of Dawn's grasp and lunged forward again with the intention of pounding, scratching and biting Derek McLaverty until he died. Dawn had restrained her just in time, but she was still only an inch from him, breathing wet rage into his ridiculously relaxed face.

'You want to hit me, Mary?' he goaded.

The answer was yes.

Several sharp nose-breaths later, Dawn managed to remove Mary from the room.

'He's an arse,' Dawn said, putting her in a taxi, 'but you won't win that way. You gotta keep the moral high ground.'

Dawn was being kind, but Mary wanted to bite her too.

24

The key's not under the mat.

She'd already honed the fantasy several times, and the taxi hadn't reached the motorway yet.

I'm not wearing my River Island boots, I am not skilled at picking locks, and I do not know for certain how to download a pen drive onto a MacBook. I find myself reading John Paul O'Donnell's court report. There's a chance he might be skilled at picking locks. I nip out, buy a disposable mobile, walk somewhere random, and dial his number.

According to the only research Mary had ever managed to get hold of, thirty percent of intrusive thoughts turn into actions. This was the case in relation to the above revenge-fantasy.

'Can you stop at Tesco, please? I'll just be a moment.' She raced in and bought a disposable mobile phone. For the rest of the journey she held her head out the window and hurled insight, consequential thinking and victim empathy to the wind. She felt better, just as the horny Zen abbot said she would.

As arranged, John Paul was waiting at the entrance to the park. She'd asked him to wear his hoodie, and she'd have pinned him as less socially acceptable than her if he'd not said: 'Fuck's sake, Mary, you look homeless as fuck. I saw online, like. Are you okay?'

'I'm fine.'

'Get rid of the bastard, Mary. I'll break his legs if I ever meet him, ruining your mouth. I admired your teeth. Women's Aid's good I hear, if you need somewhere safe. You want the number? I can totally get hold of it.'

'The pen drive's in here,' she said, showing him the bin. She'd brought rubber gloves, a torch and plastic bags, which she handed to him. 'I threw a ginger wig in there, so it'll be somewhere around that.'

In her imagination, John Paul was better at everything. It took him ages to find the pen drive, and he squealed and jumped about throughout the process. 'Why do I have to do this bit? This wasn't part of the deal. That's. Oh my God. That is not a dog shit. The animal that did this eats dogs as bar snacks. There are very large beasts in this park, Mary, very large.'

John Paul finally managed to find and clean the pen drive but would not let up about its contents.

'What's on it? Tell me, tell me. What's on it. What's on the pen drive?' He'd almost broken into song.

'None of your business. And if you look, I'll murder you.'

'You will not.'

'With my Bosch 18v.'

'Your Bosch 18v?'

'Mm-hm.'

'What's Derek McLaverty done to you, exactly, to warrant this high level of top-secret intervention?'

Mary wished she was on coke too. She was on the brink of asking him if he had any to spare; or a joint. She'd kill for a spliff. Would she ever feel free to get Johnny round again; to smoke out the window each night and feel good? 'Is this a deal or not?'

'It's a deal, and I thank you for the opportunity of it. I can repay my debts and be a free man. I can start afresh, I can move to Johnstone.' John Paul extended his hand, which had shit on it.

'Let's not shake on it just now, eh? This is the address.' She handed him a slip of paper. 'Memorise and destroy it.'

'Ha ha; memorise and destroy it.' He leaned in and whispered, 'The red fox trots quietly at midnight.'

It took John Paul a moment to realise Mary had slapped his face.

'Fuck's sake.'

'Save the files on this pen drive onto the silver MacBook on the dining table in the living room. It's the flat with the small pot plant out front. 2/2, second floor and on the right. Leave the snub on the door unlocked so it looks shut but is open, and then return the pen drive to me. And whatever you do, do not look at the files. It's financial stuff, top secret. You wouldn't understand it anyway.'

'I was good at economics.'

'You did economics?'

'No, but I was good at it. At Lowfield they called me The Bank of Saint John.'

'The Bank of Saint John, if you don't focus, I will shoot you.'

'With your Bosch 18c?'

'18v.'

'Sounds like a power tool to me.'

'Drill.'

He decided not to push it. 'So, it's the flat on your left if you're facing up the way, or down the way?'

'Facing up the way, it's the one on your right.'

He looked at the piece of paper she'd given him. 'And this

is the address, which I shall destroy. Up the way, on the right. What colour's the door? Any distinguishing features?'

He was taking the job so seriously because Mary was going to give him a hundred pounds up front and his coke buzz was waning.

'The door's blue, has a letter box thingy, a mat, and a small pot plant out front. If you look through the letterbox you'll see the dining table, and the silver MacBook open on it. Check that and you'll know you're in the right place. You can pick a lock?'

'Aye, like I said, aye! What drive?'

'What?'

'What drive you want me to save it onto?'

'I don't know!"

'I'll sort it, no worries. I'm a bit of a techy nerd, truth be told. Last week I organised my Facebook photos according to relationship, see—'

Mary didn't mean to be side-tracked, but how many women wanted to get naked with John Paul O'Donnell? There was Sylvia (2015–16), Julie (2016–17), and Cheris-An (2017–18). Julie was kinda pretty but his standards dropped after her.

He was looking at Cheris-An and it was making him morose.

'How's Christopher doing?' His profile pic was with a pal, Christopher Senior, who also happened to be one of her probationers. In the real world he wasn't known as Christopher Senior, as he was only eighteen, but that's who he was to social work. Mary had given him two hundred pounds last week to spend on whatever he wanted. In one of the extremely well-filed Facebook videos, Christopher Senior was breaking into a tennis club. Just two months ago, Christopher

Senior had been 'looked after', which meant the other end of the office cared about him and it mattered what he thought and felt. The day after his eighteenth birthday (which ended in Christopher Senior being arrested for slicing off Robert McIlhargey Junior's ear), the child-protection team booted him to Mary's end of the office with the other baddies, where he'd be punished for the rest of his life. From looked after to locked up.

Christopher Junior, nine months last week, would be looked after for the next seventeen years and three months. Poor baby; what chance did he have with a thug like Christopher Senior as a father?

'Saint John, we need to focus!'

He snapped to. 'I get four hundred once it's done?'

'Yes, to repay Kevin the Fucker. It'll be dark by two-ish so go then. And leave the door snubbed.' His expression prompted Mary to ask. 'You know what a snub is?'

'Um, dinghy.'

'Why would a rubber boat appear in this scenario?'

'Bear with me Mary. I really appreciate all this by the way, but we are failing due to cultural and translation issues. To snub means to ignore which means to dinghy in my Scotland. It's what you do when someone's a cunt, but you don't want to stab them yet. What do you do' – he lifted his arms to indicate the neat hedges of Pollokshields – 'in your Scotland?'

'I breach them.'

Recalling the precariousness of his freedom, John Paul steadied himself.

'Tell me everything I have asked you to do,' said Mary.

John Paul liked the challenge. He drew a breath before doing the opposite of summarising: 'So ... I will take this piece of paper and read it at my leisure, but well before 2.00 a.m., and then eat it.'

Although there was no need for him to eat it, she nodded. So far so good.

'Then I shall make my way to the digested address in a highly nonsuspicious manner.'

'What is it?' Mary asked.

'What?'

'The address.'

'I haven't eaten it yet!'

'Okay. Then what?'

John Paul thought very hard. 'Then I shall…' He looked for the answers in Mary's eyes, but she wasn't giving him any.

'Shit, I don't know what I'm doing,' she said.

'Ha! Me either. I thought you did!'

25

Mary had to go over the plan with John Paul seven times. Her rage and resolve did not erode with the repetition.

When she arrived home, Jack had left a note and a saucepan of chicken soup on her doorstep, both of which jarred with her state of mind.

Where are you? Been trying to ring. Geez Mum, you even managed to get the feminists to hate your guts. Holly wants you to know she didn't say those things to Derek. (You'll never be her fave person, mind – small steps ☺.) Holly and I both agree the guy's a nutter. Everything's gonna be okay, Mother-Figure, we'll work this out. Like you always say, Ma, this too shall pass.
See you in court tomorrow to #savedad
Love you,
J xx
PS: I also think you're a nutter BTW, but the good kind.

Good tingles doused the bad ones for a moment. She'd been feeling these waves since Jack was a minute old and his dark eyes chiselled into hers. It was more overwhelming that the falling-in-love swells she had in the early days with Roddie, and they were pretty intense – kept her under nine stone for three years.

What a relief. Jack was on her side. Mary put the soup on the stove.

Jack had talked to her nonstop as a toddler: 'Boigy-

boigyboigy,' he'd say, using aggressive hand gestures. She'd listen and reply in Boigy-ish, and her effort delighted him. They found other languages over the next decade, including *Thomas the Tank Engine*, *Wi*, and slingshots, briefly (Mary maimed the neighbour's cat. Jack cried for days).

Everyone with teenage boys said the same. They disappeared for a while. Mary didn't discourage it, as she often wanted to disappear herself, but had struggled to find a shared language with Jack for years now, just as *How to Bring Up Boys* had warned. At first, she tossed male role models at him in case Roddie wasn't testosteroney enough (this was mostly Roddie's worry). Her mate Brett took him fishing one day, for example, and later Mary grilled Jack – 'Tell me more about Uncle Brett!' – innocent question, innocent question, innocent question – his monosyllabic responses making her add: 'He didn't make you feel uncomfortable at any point, did he?'

'God's sake, will you let up with the paedo paranoia,' Jack said. 'So far I am the only person who wants to touch my penis.' Jack rolled his eyes, and they hadn't stopped rolling since.

She longed to talk in Boigy-ish again.

Mary reread Jack's note and poured another glass of wine. Perhaps this crisis had helped them find another shared language at last.

But no.

She was the 'good kind' before today – before she'd used an orphan to frame a misogynist. Jack thought he knew who she was, and he didn't. He thought she was the good kind and she wasn't.

Fuck that. Derek McLaverty needed to be stopped. She put the letter in her *special things* box, turned the soup off because it wouldn't go well with the wine, and took the latter with her to bed.

Bugger, she'd cut the cord of her laptop and it was out of charge. How would this work without *Sex and the City*? How would she get to sleep without the comfort of the girls, shouting about how they felt? *This is how I feel! Fuck you if you don't like it – choose* any *other show on any other channel. This is how it feels.*

She woke to a clang. It was dark, 2.50 a.m. Mary opened the blind in the kitchen and, sure enough, someone was at the bins. She grabbed a knife in case it was Jimmy McKinley again, this time with a plan. As she headed downstairs it dawned on her that McKinley would get away with it now, but hell, that happened most of the time, and it eased the blow knowing how hard he'd worked on his 'child love' collection, how much he'd miss it, and that there was nothing he could do about it. She'd racked her brain – there was nothing he could do about it.

As Mary walked across the back green she knew she was heading towards danger but continued anyway. The figure she was heading for was definitely John Paul O'Donnell, but someone was behind him.

'We met by chance,' John Paul said, 'and he insisted on coming. Sorry. He didn't believe me about the money you owe me … for the…'

'Sofa,' Mary said.

'Aye.'

'Did you fit it through the door?' she asked.

'What door?' John Paul must've already spent the hundred she gave him. He was wasted.

'I take it you're Kevin the Fucker,' Mary said.

'You can call me Kevin.'

His name suited him. Mary handed over four hundred pounds.

'I'm in the furniture business too,' said Kevin the Fucker. 'If you're ever looking for a sofa, I'm the wholesale guy. Don't go retail, like to this knob.'

Poor John Paul, he was even despised by the person he paid a hundred pounds a day (if times were good).

As Kevin the Fucker counted the money, John Paul slipped the pen drive into her hand. It was still hot.

'Thank you,' said Mary, 'but I'm okay seating-wise just now.'

Kevin the Fucker winked and jotted his number on a bus ticket. 'This is my mobile. If you're texting, just say how many. For example: *Hey Kevin, you got any two-seaters?* Or: *Hi Kevin, I'm looking for a three-seater.*'

'Or: *Hello, I would like a four-seater sofa please.*' John Paul added. 'That's code for four grams of cocaine.'

Kevin the Fucker rolled his eyes at John Paul the Ned.

'I don't need any sofas at the moment,' she said to Kevin the Fucker. 'But thanks.'

With the deal closed, John Paul scaled the wall, while his dealer chose to exit via the gate.

I'm gonna have to move. Mary closed the back door to the garden. *I'm gonna lose my beautiful home.*

In her left hand, Mary clamped the pen drive with plyers. With her right she drilled at the small piece of metal and plastic, shaving at the edges and repositioning until the device settled as dust on her newly holey bread board.

Some dust was on her finger. She wondered how many ruined lives were now stuck to the sweat on the top of her finger. Mary downed a glass of kitchen Sangiovese for courage because there was no time for this kind of thinking.

She put on her hoodie.

She looked for her personal mobile – shite, she'd destroyed her phone. There'd be no 'Kickass' playlist in the next scenario. She put her enormous headphones on anyway, to give the impression of kickass.

Mary walked somewhere random (the pond at Maxwell Park) and made an anonymous call to the police with the disposable mobile she'd bought. The husky voice she used totally worked with the trench coat and River Island boots.

'Hello,' she croaked when she was finally put through to the Offender Management Unit. 'This is an anonymous referral from an anonymous source regarding Derek McLaverty. No, I will not. No, I will not tell you who I am. Okay, fuck.' She hung up and rang 101, the non-emergency 999, and was happy to have reached someone who had no choice but to listen.

'This is anonymous,' she said. 'My friend's friend, Derek McLaverty, who's staying at 2/1 3908 Pollokshaws Road, Shawlands ... My um, my friend, who also wishes to remain anonymous for reasons you will see, was at the above address about a week ago and she, I mean, *he*, said DEREK MCLAVERTY' (then she spelt it out) 'was bragging about some stuff he's got online and it was right dodgy.' Mary was trying to sound unprofessional but needn't have bothered as she'd forgotten how to sound otherwise. 'So, my friend said he showed my pal these pictures on his silver MacBook that made him vomit, actually hurl, like. He said there were little children in sexual … situations. She saw it, on his laptop, and was proper shaken, so I said I had to tell, so that's what I'm doing. Derek McLaverty's his name. Load of stuff on his MacBook unless he's gotten rid of it. He's twenty-nine and lives…'

She gave the Shawlands address again and hung up.

Mary threw the mobile away and headed home, smiling, because Derek McLaverty was now the scum of the earth.

No-one would hear him roar now.

26

When Mary got back from the park, around 4.30 a.m., Jimmy McKinley was standing on the pavement staring up at her windows. Being doxed was a serious pain in the arse.

'Oi!'

He started walking away, but Mary caught up with him. 'Get the fuck away from my house.'

'I will when you give it back to me, Mary.' Without his Zimmer he'd lost about twenty years and gained a whole heap of sinister.

'Give what back?'

'You're enjoying it, aren't you? Isn't it incredible watching them grow? Little V's my favourite. Don't you love Little V? Nice to find a kindred spirit in you, Mary, but it's mine, and I'd like it back now.'

'I'm calling the police.' Mary raced to her door and eventually managed to get inside. Little V? Who was Little V? Not Vanny, please not Vanny.

Having given up thinking for several hours now, she felt comfortable being drawn along by impulses, the strongest of which was to fashion twenty flyers, using flipchart paper and an assortment of felt-tip pens.

WARNING!
JIMMY MCKINLEY

WHO LIVES AT NO 2 MASON COURT IS A
REGISTERED SEX OFFENDER!
HE HAS A CHILD SEX ROBOT.
HE SEXUALLY ASSAULTED HIS FIVE-
YEAR-OLD DAUGHTER.
HE HAS BEEN DOWNLOADING
CHILD ABUSE FOR YEARS.
PLEASE KEEP YOUR CHILDREN SAFE

She finished her glass of wine, drove to Mason Court and posted the flyers in his neighbour's doors. Every second house had a dog, so Mary ran as fast as she could, slipping flyers into postboxes, sticking one on the bus stop and another on the community noticeboard. She drove four blocks to Vanny's flat, and posted one in her door, just in case she was Little V. Everyone would start waking soon, and she felt confident the community would respond speedily. By morning, Jimmy McKinley's house would be spray-painted *Beast! Paedo! Keep your Children Safe!* by the local vigilantes, who'd driven three of Mary's Nasties out over the years. Bricks would be tossed through his windows. By lunchtime, he'd have packed his bags and snuck out the back door, never to be seen again.

To think, she was going to let him get away with it.

Jack was in the hall when she arrived home.

'Mum, where have you been? This place is a mess. What have you been doing? Your tooth. Are you okay? Oh my God, did Dad do that to you?' He burst into tears. 'What's that flipchart all about? You're not doing anything stupid, are you? What's happening, Mum, I'm scared.'

'It's okay, baby, everything's okay.' Nothing was better than hugging her son, comforting him, but her tears were not supporting her assertion.

'Mum, I can't find Holly.'

Good, a problem to sort. Mary wiped her face and blew her nose. 'Is there any reason to be worried?'

'Remember those unpublished letters you found the day of the launch? Well she hadn't read them, till a couple of hours ago, that is. In most of them he's just way less charming, but these two – read them.' He handed her the first letter.

Dearest Bella,

In visits this morning, Holly offered to get us coffee at the kiosk. I was glad to sit alone for a moment and was already longing for the respite of my cell. Despite saying nothing, we had already run out of things to say. I was thinking about our first meal together, Bella. You asked me to book a restaurant, so I chose an expensive one. When the bill came, the waiter gave it to me, and you let him. It was ten pounds less than the total in my account, and my rent was due. I felt sick for a moment and smiled at you for help. You blushed and turned your head. It surprised me, Bella, that you made a binding contract at that moment, signed and tipped, when it was exactly what you railed against. But you never railed too hard, did you? You were a champagne feminist, and I had to buy the champagne.

Holly spilt coffee on the way back to the table and I was overcome with hatred. Your daughter was the exception to the rule. I was authentic with her. I trusted her.

You should never have asked her to keep a secret from me, but Holly should never have agreed. Her lie was worse than yours, Bella. I nearly threw boiling coffee in her face. Maybe next time I will.

Liam

'This one's worse,' Jack said, handing her the second letter.

Dear Bella,
I shouldn't be writing this now as I'm moody. Holly always leaves me feeling moody.

It's the eat-it-too blast radius again. It has taken her in, as well as thousands of others. Some of the ripples have been so big they've made their own blast, and I am afraid Holly may be one of them.

She was always glum, was she not? Probably because we didn't buy her any dolls. She reminds me of you, Bella, when you were at your worst, which was always, in the end. Crying one minute, laughing the next. Needy-whiney-needy then all don't-mess-with-me. She wants me to live with her when I get out. The very thought! She visits every week, and I wish she wouldn't. How can I look at her, Bella, when I also wanted her dead?

I'm having negative thoughts and Julie has warned me not to have these. It's because of Holly. I might take her name off my visitor's list.

Liam

Jack folded the letters with shaky hands. 'She was supposed to go for oysters that day.'
'Who?'
'Holly. Her parents were fighting in the car, she got out

at a red light and walked home. Her father yelled "GET IN THE CAR! GET IN THE CAR!" for ages but she kept walking.'

'And…'

'She hears him yell that in her sleep. She's always blamed herself, see, thinks if she went like she was supposed to it never would have happened. But her dad didn't snap. He made a plan, and the only thing that went wrong was that Holly got out of the car.'

'The poor girl,' Mary said. 'I'm not surprised, though.'

'It surprised Holly. She's not answering her phone.'

'We've got a few hours till court,' Mary said. 'You go to hers and wait in case she comes back. I'll check the cemetery.'

'Of course. Okay. I love you, Mum.' Jack hugged her at the door.

They were talking! The wave of tingles! 'I love you too, my baby boy.'

She heard the girl before she saw her, howling 'Mum! Mum! Where are you?' Her voice was coming from the spooky section, where gnarled trees had grown wild and now encased the gothic monuments. This place was cobwebby and shadowy; magical and scary; overgrown foliage in bright, jumping LSD greens. Mary, Roddie and Jack used to do ghost tours here, taking turns to scare the shit out of each other.

She walked past headstones that had toppled face down into the cloggy earth. No-one was alive to maintain the memorials of Archibald Jamieson and Margaret Thom and Eleanor McWilliams. Their names would be mud for eternity. Mary walked to the top of the hill, taking in the view of compact, sensible Glasgow, its mountain edges visible from every angle. There was Holly, running on the soft grass between the lines of the long dead, checking each name as she ran, frantic and sobbing.

When she spotted Mary, she howled: 'I can't find her. I've been looking for hours. She's gone.' She pushed an overgrown shrub off an epitaph. 'I don't remember where she is.'

It was raining, and Holly's hair and clothes were drenched. Mary wrapped a jumper around her shoulders. 'She won't be here, hon. Come, the new part's over there.'

They walked in silence across to the new section, a grassy woodland path encasing them then clearing to reveal a sea of new dead. Mary worked methodically, and they found Holly's mother's plaque in the eighteenth row.

ISABELLA DUFF
BELOVED MOTHER OF HOLLY

Holly fell to her knees, crying. She brushed mud from her mother's name: 'Beloved mother.'

Mary found herself crying too and knelt on the wet grass beside the girl. 'What was she like?'

Holly always thought hard before answering a question, a skill Mary peddled but did not have. 'I'm looking forward to remembering.' She considered the question again. 'Energetic. She was energetic. Always had to have five things to look forward to. That was her rule. Five things to look forward to.' Holly had brought yellow roses, which she placed on the plaque. She stood again and wiped her tears. 'Where am I supposed to bury him?'

'You're gonna get a cold. Come on.' Mary took Holly's

arm and began walking back to the car. 'You could cremate him – scatter his ashes on the Braes, above Castlemilk. In one of his letters he said he was happy there, as a child.'

Holly thought about it and nodded.

The heavens opened, huge thick droplets like the ones they get in nice warm places.

'Wanna run for it?' Mary said.

'Not really.' But Holly had taken off already.

When they arrived at Holly's, Jack was waiting on the step. The two of them were still embracing when Mary turned the corner.

27

Mary managed to make herself look human in time for court, but it turned out to be quite a complicated process. The glue she'd used on her tooth had turned dark brown. No matter how hard she scrubbed, she could not restore its original colour. She'd have to keep her mouth shut at all times. She practised in the mirror, pursing her lips and saying 'Yes, your honour! Mary Shields, twenty Mansion House Square, your honour!' It was a tad blow-jobby. Hopefully, Mary would not need to talk in court.

In the shower she noticed quite a few injuries that she could not explain. If the police saw the state of her, Roddie would never get out. There was a huge gash on her ankle, and fresh blood trickled into the drain. She had a cut on her foot, scratch marks on her calves and neck, and a range of bruises on her thighs and shoulders.

She weighed 9st 8lb. She'd lost four pounds. Mary retrieved her long forgotten 9st 8lb trousers and drove to court.

The protestors outside Renfield Sheriff Court seemed the same shape and size as at Lowfield on the day of Liam Macdowall's release. (Was that really eleven days ago?) There were forty or so men. About twenty women. They didn't chant, and only a few of them carried standard-issue placards. The men did not wear t-shirts with the letter C. The women did not hate Mary. Everyone seemed tired, and a little confused. It seemed to Mary that the men and women only separated to clear a path for her.

On the way in, service-providers, or people, as Mary preferred to call them, handed her their cards – Assist, Victim Support, Women's Aid. There were no official services for the likes of Roddie. Mary tried hard to avoid McLaverty's velvet-suited lawyer, but he accosted her outside court four.

'Listen, Mary, sorry and all that. I'm an arsehole – it's my job. Can we talk shop? I'm here for John Paul O'Donnell.'

'He's in court?'

'Down in the cells; custody court. He walked in the station early this morning asking to be arrested. Convinced five officers, eventually. The usual: got his hands on some money, too much coke, can't recall a thing. Will you root for him? Give him another shot?'

'Of course I will,' Mary said. 'CPO et cetera; you name it.' She'd do anything, in fact, because it was her fault.

She took a seat behind Adeela and Roddie, whose body remained steadfastly facing forwards, and who tapped his fingers on the bench.

Adeela turned around as mediator. 'He's pleading guilty.'

'What?'

'What the hell have you done with that tooth?' Adeela lowered to a whisper. 'Is that ... is that also tooth? What is that in between? Why is it brown? Keep your mouth closed.' She sniffed. 'Have you showered?'

She had. Had she done it badly?

Roddie was too intrigued not to turn around.

She opened wide and grinned. She always won him over that way, by being entertaining.

He suppressed a laugh, then frowned. 'I am so sorry. Oh my God, Mary. Sorry and guilty. Can you forgive me?'

'Of course.' She pressed her forehead on his, but it didn't feel as good as it usually did, and she separated before it became a thing.

'Listen, Jack just phoned,' Adeela said. 'Said he might be a few minutes late. He had to pass by Holly's dad's cos he left—'

The wigged guy had entered.

'ALL STAND.'

Perhaps she bowed too fast? Her chair caught her when she fell back. She kept her head between her legs as the fiscal and Adeela muttered their cases. In for four, hold for seven. Sweat was dripping down her neck. She lifted her head slowly and tapped Adeela on the shoulder: 'What did Jack leave? Why isn't he here?'

'Quiet, please.' Sheriff Mackay had always hated Mary. (What does "criminogenic need" mean?' he'd demanded a few years back. Mary despised the jargon too, but she did know what it meant – 'What Rab needs to stop slitting relatives' throats,' she'd said. 'And what exactly does "sex as coping" mean?' Sheriff Mackay had demanded to know a year or so ago. 'Ejaculating to cheer up,' she'd said. 'Which is usually fine in my opinion.')

'How do you plead, Mr Lawson?' said today's Sheriff Mackay.

'Guilty, your honour.'

Mary wondered if he'd pled thus due to the five-syllable thing; surely not.

Sheriff Mackay raised his eyebrows at Roddie. 'Your lawyer has outlined significant mitigating circumstances…'

'I hit my wife, your honour. I'm guilty.'

Sheriff Mackay looked like he was having intrusive thoughts involving hitting Mary.

She tried to relax: there was a seventy percent chance this would not turn to action.

The sheriff sighed – another lost cause, this Roderick Lawson – and Mary could almost see him fantasy-hammer her skull into the mahogany desk. 'One hundred hours unpaid work, to be completed within six months.'

The next moment was a good one. She held Roddie, and everything was okay.

That was it, over. Two seconds at most, it was, her head in his chest, his arms sticking her back together.

They had to clear the court room in preparation for the likes of John Paul O'Donnell, whose overdose Mary had financed.

Only three protestors remained outside, and they were packing to head off too. Adeela walked them to the car, and Mary wondered the entire time if it was to see if she could walk straight. She *so* could.

'Why was Jack going to Macdowall's this morning?' she asked Adeela when they reached the car.

'Oh, to get his laptop.'

'What?'

'He said he left it at her dad's last week.'

'Jack did? Where?'

'Liam Macdowall's.'

'His laptop?'

'Tablet, I don't know.'

'What colour? Silver?' Fight mode: on.

'Why the hell would I know?' said Adeela.

28

Mary pushed to the front of the queue at the court. 'Sorry, sorry, it's urgent.'

She grabbed her bag and ID from the scanner and ran downstairs to the cells. A dungeon, it was, guarded by the World's Unhappiest Officer. 'I need to see John Paul O'Donnell,' Mary said.

He would not be distracted from the *Daily Mail*. Mary knew there was only one way to get what she wanted. She put her ID on his desk and waited for him to pretend to finish reading his article. Eventually, he folded his paper and walked nonchalantly towards the cells.

'Booth one,' he called back.

John Paul's eyes were red, his face grey. He took his seat on the opposite side of the glass and stared at the floor. He was expecting help, no doubt, as he had all his life. He was sitting there expecting her to fix things for him.

Mary waited till the officer was back at his desk. 'What computer did you put it on?'

'The silver one,' said John Paul.

'Where was it?'

'On the table in the living room.'

'Was there another computer in the house?'

'Didn't look.'

Palpitations; holy shit, she could hear them. She had no time for palpitations now. 'Jesus Christ, John Paul, do you ever do anything right? Your poor grandpa must be turning in his grave. Fuck, you idiot; you pea-brained useless fucking ned.'

He was crying when she stood, and for all of two seconds she didn't give a toss.

'I'm so, so sorry,' she said. 'I didn't mean any of that.'

Did she though?

'I really didn't mean any of it. And whatever happens, I'll keep you out of it, I promise.'

She ran right past Roddie and Adeela, who'd been waiting for her outside the court.

'Gotta go, Adeela, thanks for everything. Roddie, come with me – quick – I'll explain in the car.'

But she didn't explain in the car. There was still a chance she might not need to. So she lied instead. 'I was having a panic about Jack,' she said. 'I just need to check he's okay.'

The service buzzer let them in, and Mary prayed as she took two steps at a time: *Please God. Please God. Please God.* She knew her prayers were no good – they never had been – when she saw the open door and heard a man talking. She ran inside Liam Macdowall's flat and stopped dead in the hall. Jack was sitting at the dining table opposite Detective Sergeant Minnie Johnstone and a colleague Mary had never met. Her baby boy was sobbing.

He was under arrest, Minnie explained, for downloading abusive images. They were taking him into custody, and he'd appear in court tomorrow.

But Mary could explain. 'Listen, Minnie, please. The images are Jimmy McKinley's.'

'What?'

'I found a pen drive in his house. I was going to get it to

you – I left you a message? But you will not believe the week I've been having.'

Minnie asked her to take a seat and gave her a glass of water. 'And where is the pen drive?'

'I destroyed it, with my drill. I thought this was Derek McLaverty's MacBook. I downloaded the pen drive onto it, then I destroyed the drive.'

'Mary, take a breath,' Minnie said.

Roddie was tapping his fingers so loudly. 'Take a breath, baby.' He thought she was mad. That would be so much better.

'How did you get into this flat?' asked Minnie.

'I broke in.'

'Oh yeah. How'd you break in?' said Minnie.

'I'm telling the truth. I wish I wasn't. I put it on Derek's MacBook, which I assumed was this one, to stop him. He's ruining our lives. Minnie, this has nothing to do with Jack. I did it. Don't arrest him and make him go to court. Please believe me. It's true. The press will be all over this at court even if it's dismissed. No matter what, Jack will be all over the internet as a paedophile.' Everyone was ignoring her. 'Please listen to me, Minnie.'

Minnie sighed and relaxed, which made Mary do the same.

'I understand, Mary. He's your son. You and Roddie are his parents. You'll be in his life forever.'

Mary nuzzled her son's head into her chest. He was having difficulty breathing and couldn't stop crying.

'You want to know what was on it, Mary? Remember Fred – we coworked on him five years back? Remember the stuff he liked to look at? Well the images on your son's computer make Fred's baby-plus-cats series look like *Mary Poppins*. Am

I right in thinking you've just been sentenced for domestic assault?' she asked Roddie.

'Yes.' He was staring at the floor the way John Paul did.

'And that you had an affair with your client?' she asked Mary. Minnie was doing a risk assessment on the entire family, and it was not coming out well.

'No, I didn't. That was a lie, ask Holly.'

'You're a denier?' said Minnie, who was once lovely enough to be Minnie Mouse. 'Everyone hates a denier.' She grabbed Jack's arm, forcing him to stand, and began reading him his rights.

'Jack,' Mary said, 'I am telling the truth. I did this. I can get you out of it.'

'Really? If it is the truth, no-one is ever going to believe it. Did you really? Did you really do that?' Jack was not going down with dignity. Mary tried to wipe his nose with a tissue, but he pulled away. 'What did you do, Mum? What the fuck did you do to me?'

Mary turned to Holly, stony-faced at the kitchen door. 'Holly. It's a crazy story, I know. You know me. Tell the police – I'm a fucking lunatic. You have to believe me.'

Holly kept her arms folded and thought about her answer before giving it: 'You know me, Mary, I believe anything.'

The other officer packed away the MacBook and all Jack's other belongings. They were ready to take him away.

'You're the fucking blast, Mum,' Jack sobbed as they walked him to the door. 'You're the fucking blast and I'm just another of your fucking ripples.'

Before Minnie left the flat, she turned back and said: 'Mary, I won't tell your bosses the state of you today, but my advice is you avoid covering up for him, eh? Just makes him seem even creepier.' She pushed Jack's head and followed him out the door, shouting back one last thing: 'And don't call me Minnie.'

—

Jack stared ahead till the police van doors slammed shut. He looked like he'd gone into shock.

'You are a weapon of mass destruction,' Roddie said, watching the van disappear.

'Do you believe me, though?'

'You've ruined his life.' Roddie was crying. 'You've ruined his life.'

No, she hadn't. She'd fix this. She'd make a plan.

'Listen. I'm gonna head home,' said Holly, pale-faced and depleted. She gave Mary a look that could only mean goodbye and headed down the road.

An action plan began to form in the air, as if Mary had a flipchart and a pen that worked. 'I'll sort this,' she said to Roddie, who was dumbstruck.

Action 1: Ensure Jack's safety.

She dialled Govan Police Station. 'Hi Herb! I believe you've got Jack Shields-Lawson arriving soon? How's Alice by the way?'

'Ach she's a winner. Three on Saturday!'

'Three! Doesn't it fly in? This is unusual, but Jack Shields-Lawson – I'm his mum, Herb. He's my baby. Can you check on him? Make sure he's okay? Tell him I'm fixing things and not to worry. There's been a terrible mistake.'

'Will do.'

Action 2: Lawyer him up.

She dialled Adeela. 'Mary here … Oh you've heard already? Can you get to Govan? Take him some money, tell him I'll visit him wherever he is after work. Jack Shields-Lawson, his date of birth is … What?'

Adeela did not wish to take the case and had hung up before Mary could say 'fuck you'. She realised she was still standing on the pavement outside Macdowall's flat, and Roddie was still staring at her.

'Oh my God, Mary. I was gone a week.'

There was no time for this conversation. Mary was talking to another lawyer, and then to Karen, in case Jack ended up at Lowfield. She hung up when she realised Roddie was chanting.

'I have to get out.' He shook his arms, as if Mary had been stuck on them. 'I have to get out,' he said, and backed away.

29

She put the Sat Nav on because she couldn't do it on her own, even though she'd driven this route at least twice a day for the last thirty years.

—*At the end of the road, turn left...*

When was the moment? she thought. *When did I make the choice that ended here? Was it when I wanked thinking about Macdowall?*

—*At the roundabout, take the second exit, Renfield...*

Was it when I did a home visit to McKinley on my own? Which one? The first with the doll, or the second with the pen drive? She wasn't supposed to do home visits to sex offenders on her own, for reasons she now understood, but there was never anyone available to come with her. If she'd waited around till someone could, she'd have been in trouble way before now.

—*At the roundabout, take the third exit, Renfield...*

Small decisions, all of them, but one of them set things off.

—*In two hundred metres, turn right, Mason Court...*

As she turned, she spotted Jimmy McKinley's bungalow. The front door was open. *Paedo* and *Beast* had been spray-painted on the pebbledash and door, and at least one window was broken. He'd fled, obviously. Underground now, with no supervision whatsoever. Mary had made him more dangerous.

—*In two hundred metres, turn left, Grange Road...*

Thank God she had the meeting in ten minutes: to be

in a room with qualified listeners, to be comforted, have things clarified, decisions made. She couldn't leave the job now, not with Roddie unemployed. She couldn't take any more sick leave because she was stage four now, probably, which meant something very bad. Her flexitime had been swallowed again, she had no holidays owing, and no money to buy extra leave. She had to fight to stay in this place. She had to find a way to cope. She must not let anything set her off again.

—You have reached your destination.

Mary pulled up outside the office and rummaged for change in her grotty car. There was a parking meter epidemic in Renfield, even though very few residents drove a car – not their own, anyway. She'd tossed her fury to the wind re parking years ago, but it boomeranged now as she scraped a twenty-pence piece from the floor and picked off the brown substance coating it. She had to pay? In this wasteland, near a sewage plant. Where no-one even had a car except the council army that had long occupied the area – the Stasi soldiers who paced the High Street at lunchtime, lanyards swinging from their necks. She counted out two quid in silver, put it in the meter, and opened the boot. Tuna was plentiful – no-one wanted that – but she was running low on baked beans and UHT milk. As usual for the last week or two, she left the boot open, and stuck her laminated *PLEASE HELP YOURSELF* sign on the number plate.

Mary was vibrating, she was an enormous walking Just Ears. Her son had just been arrested for downloading abusive images of children. Right now, he was handcuffed in the back of a van. To the drivers, he was the scum of the earth. In prison, he'd be abused and beaten. In court tomorrow, men's rights activists and *Renfield Star* journalists would jot down details to embellish and spread. Online, he'd be the evil monster we must all watch out for. He'd have to register every year. He wouldn't be allowed to have his dog. Marty! He wouldn't be allowed to have Marty. The law firm would sack him. If found guilty, he'd never practise law, or get any kind of job, ever. He wouldn't be allowed near children and if he went near a woman, social work would put a stop to it. He'd go to groupwork with the likes of Jimmy McKinley, and maybe he'd learn a thing or two, make some pals.

She stopped before the front doors because she couldn't breathe. 'I must not think about that. I must not think about that,' she repeated, definitely out loud, because a skinny client was offering her a cigarette.

He lit it for her.

His kindness, as well as the deep, smoky breathing, calmed her. She had arrived at the right place, the concrete box she'd worked in for thirty years, where chaos was expected and unhappiness the currency, where she was the goody who worked with the baddies, where poverty made her feel rich and despair made her feel blessed, where her colleagues were her mates, her boss her confidante, and where crises always blew over.

Management didn't know she'd done anything wrong. To her colleagues and bosses, her client had committed suicide, which was a pain in the arse and would involve months of scrutiny on every level, but was nothing unusual. She'd been doxed and trolled, which was shitty, but not her fault. And she'd have to prove she didn't shag Macdowall, but she reckoned she could do that – maybe using the location device on her laptop or phone, or something, or asking Holly to make a statement. There had to be a way.

As for Jack, Mary needed time to think up a more

believable story than the truth. The bosses had dealt with this kind of thing many times. Last year Alice Belmont's son killed his mate after a drunken game of quoits turned nasty. Alice, a children-and-families social worker, was restricted from all information pertaining to her son, but otherwise she was unscathed. She took the last drag of her cigarette and stubbed it out.

The automatic doors opened. 'Hi Nel,' she said to the receptionist.

Nel was on the phone and gave a weak wave.

In the waiting room, there were two Mental Mothers – one shaking, one crying – with their three Kids at Risk.

'Hey gorgeous!' Mary said to Kid at Risk One, whose name was either Chloe or Zoe.

'I have juice,' Kid at Risk One said, and Mary was excited too. Chloe or Zoe didn't often get juice.

Beside Mental Mother One was an out-of-place thirty-something man – interpreter, Polish, probably, as the Poles were the only migrants to have willingly settled in the area since 1900. Opposite him, a middle-aged woman grasped her designer bag (divorce, drink driving). An elderly heroin-user rocked on the seat next to her. (All heroin-users were elderly. This one deserved an award for still being alive.) Mary smiled at the Heroin-User, the lowest of the low, or almost. Junkie: an unspeakably dirty word.

Mr Angry in the corner was seething cos he had to come to this fucking place. *I hate you*, he was saying to Mary with his whole face, and Mary's whole face was saying: *Not as much as I hate you*.

And there was a guy in the telephone-box-sized room next to Nel. He'd been put there for safety reasons. Everyone knew this was the equivalent of the naughty step; that he was either a paedophile or a rapist. Rapist, Mary had decided straight away. He almost filled the entire booth and looked rapey as fuck. The glass had fogged up and he'd drawn a love heart on the steamy window, making Kids at Risk One and Three cry.

Jack might end up sitting in this blowhole of a reception, Mary thought. He'd be the one in the kennel, everyone looking in, everyone – even Mr Rapist, Mr Junkie and Mental Mother Two, who had just vomited in the plastic bin – would look at Jack and feel better because they were not the lowest of the low after all.

She pressed her ID against the machine. Minus seventeen hours, it said. She stared at it a long time. Minus seventeen hours. She took the stairs to the first floor.

The hangar-like space was heavy with Monday-ness, which was the saddest day of the social worker's week. Weekends always failed to deliver, and workers wore the disbelief on their faces all day. *I am back here already. This is my life. This is all I do and I hate it.*

It was 3.50 p.m. Mary walked past the community service pod, where Keith was enjoying his power on the phone: 'You got to the food bank, yeah, yeah? If you can get there, Michael, you can get to your unpaid work, see what I'm saying? No, no, let me speak. No, that's a final warning, Michael.' She tried to catch Keith's eye, but didn't manage. He might talk to Roddie that way, she thought.

Her pod was empty, bar the pile of papers on her chair.

She spotted Lil exiting at the childcare end of the room. Lil was here, thank God. Or had she seen Mary first and pelted? News might well have reached the office about Jack's arrest. Minnie might have phoned Catherine, who might have messaged Lil. In for four, hold for seven, out for eight. She had too much to fix and must repel the red mist.

The papers on her chair included a new life licence, which Mary scanned. Iain Sanderson, who'd raped and murdered three elderly women in 1987, 1988 and 2007. She had been allocated five court reports: assault, drink driving, drugs, stalking, one for racist prick Simon Gallacher and one for Derek McLaverty (bail act, domestic assault).

She put her head between her legs for a moment, then opened the window to take in some sewage air. A moment later the desire to smash everything in the room subsided a little, and she returned to the complaint against McLaverty.

After returning from the Edinburgh Book Festival, he had turned up at his in-law's house to see his boys and banged on the door till his ex-wife came outside. He was found guilty of breaching bail, pulling her hair, punching her in the face and throwing a large rock at her back. Whoever allocated the report was blissfully clueless. Mary would ask to have this report reassigned.

If Jack was found guilty, one of her colleagues would get a report request like Derek's. Lil, maybe. Or Sylvia. Whoever it was would scan the paperwork as Mary just had, see his name and age and crime and think: *Agh. Gross. Arsehole.*

She also had about thirty telephone messages, many from people she didn't know or couldn't remember, and seventy-two emails, none of which looked terrifying at first glance.

She was starting to feel less unsafe.

Catherine wasn't in her office, which meant the meeting would be downstairs, and that Mary would have to do the walk of shame. She braced herself and made the journey she had made thousands of times, past Sylvia in criminal justice, who'd usually look up to say hi, but didn't today; past the children-and-families workers who were busy praying *Please don't let me ruin a child today. Please do not let me ruin a child.* None of them acknowledged Mary because news had obviously already spread. She was a walking nightmare. *Behold Mary*, they were all thinking – *and never, ever take the mother's word for it.*

Because Mary *had* ruined a child's life today. Her own.

She was dizzy when she reached the opposite door, and only made it halfway down the stairs before needing to sit. A moment later, the door behind her banged. Footsteps. Someone was coming.

'Mary!'

Fuck, it was the green-haired student social worker. Mary didn't have her headphones, shit. She decided it was best to make a dash.

'Mary, stop!' The girl had caught up with her. Her hand was on Mary's arm. 'You're shaky. You're going to fall over. Stop. Sit for a minute.'

Mary collapsed onto a step and blurted out: 'There are no programmes of offence-focused work for autistic gamblers. I'd just have to make it up, and it'd take ages, and I don't want to. I don't want to help you.'

The student social worker was holding her. How did that happen? 'I heard about your son. I'm so sorry.'

'He didn't—'

'I know. Of course he didn't. I know. I believe you. It's okay. If anyone can get through this, you can. You're amazing. Here.' She took Mary's hand and pulled her upright. 'Where are you heading? I'll take you.'

The conference room stank of the power of senior social workers. Catherine, her boss and confidante, sat at the far end of the enormous table, and gave Mary a nervous smile. Beside her was her boss's boss, Shirley, whose presence made Mary hot and itchy.

She had to hold it together for Jack. 'Can you give me a moment?' She concentrated. 'I'm having a panic attack. Just a moment...' *Four, seven, eight,* she repeated three times, even though she didn't feel much better, then began contemplating the daunting task of lifting her head.

'Mary? Mary,' Shirley said. 'Are you okay?'

The table had morphed into the one at Lowfield, and Jack was surrounded by officers and social workers:

You will not. You may not. You must not. Without the prior permission of your supervising officer.

'Mary!' Shirley was starting to sound mean. This often happened with Shirley.

Was that the red mist rising? It felt red. But it felt more ominous than mist.

'I understand you've been going through, well, a lot, but this is a very serious situation, Mary, and we felt we really shouldn't postpone.'

Shirley kept talking, but Mary couldn't hear for the terrible snippets invading, making her dizzy again:

I made an excellent decision today. I beat up a paedophile.

She imagined Derek McLaverty kicking Jack in his cell, smashing her bleeding boy's skull.

You're the blast and I'm just another of your fucking ripples!

She imagined Jack having dinner in D hall, chatting away with Jimmy McKinley and Robert the Rapist.

'I must not think about that,' Mary said, which made Shirley stop talking and Catherine look up.

Her calves were itchy and she had to scratch.

'As I was saying...' Shirley swept a piece of paper across the table for Mary to peruse. It was filled with numbers, which began to blur, swirl and redden. 'The dates we've highlighted,' Shirley said, 'are the days you arrived outwith core hours or left within core hours. Thirty-three times since Christmas, Mary.'

She finally managed to lift her whirling, leaden head. She looked at the spreadsheet, then at her boss, then at her boss's boss, then at her boss again, and said: 'This meeting is about flexitime?'

Acknowledgements

Thanks to:

Karen Sullivan, my bold and inspiring editor.

My agent, Phil Patterson, for his faith, loveliness and hard work.

Gill and Michelle, for their friendship and feedback.

The brilliant Luke Speed at Curtis Brown.

Lisa O'Donnell and Robyn Wilson for reading early drafts and giving incredible notes.

And to HRT, which got me out of bed to write this book. If Mary had slapped on a patch, none of this would ever have happened.